KING

COBRA

Lisa,
So great to see
you at RAGT22!
Jayne
Rylon

JAYNE RYLON

eBook ISBN: 978-1-941785-34-8
Print ISBN: 978-1-941785-65-2

Ebook Cover Art By Angela Waters
Print Book Cover Art By Jayne Rylon
Interior Print Book Design By Jayne Rylon

Sign Up For The Naughty News!
Contests, sneak peeks, appearance info, and more.
www.jaynerylon.com/newsletter

Shop
Autographed books, reading-themed apparel,
notebooks, totes, and more.
www.jaynerylon.com/shop

Contact Jayne
Email: contact@jaynerylon.com
Website: www.jaynerylon.com
Facebook: Facebook.com/JayneRylon
Twitter: @JayneRylon

OTHER BOOKS BY JAYNE RYLON

<u>DIVEMASTERS</u>
Going Down
Going Deep
Going Hard

<u>MEN IN BLUE</u>
Night is Darkest
Razor's Edge
Mistress's Master
Spread Your Wings
Wounded Hearts
Bound For You

<u>POWERTOOLS</u>
Kate's Crew
Morgan's Surprise
Kayla's Gift
Devon's Pair
Nailed to the Wall
Hammer it Home

HOTRODS
King Cobra
Mustang Sally
Super Nova
Rebel on the Run
Swinger Style
Barracuda's Heart
Touch of Amber
Long Time Coming

COMPASS BROTHERS
Northern Exposure
Southern Comfort
Eastern Ambitions
Western Ties

COMPASS GIRLS
Winter's Thaw
Hope Springs
Summer Fling
Falling Softly

PLAY DOCTOR
Dream Machine
Healing Touch

STANDALONES
4-Ever Theirs
Nice & Naughty
Where There's Smoke
Report For Booty

RACING FOR LOVE
Driven
Shifting Gears

RED LIGHT
Through My Window
Star
Can't Buy Love
Free For All

PARANORMALS
Picture Perfect
Reborn
PICK YOUR PLEASURES
Pick Your Pleasure
Pick Your Pleasure 2

DEDICATION

For everyone who's gotten a speeding ticket. Especially if you really deserved it.

Also to Ivelisse Roberts, Kim Rocha and Pilar Cruz for making sure I curse like an authentic Cuban. I love the random skills I develop as an author!

CHAPTER ONE

Eli London stared at the drop of sweat gathering on the shoulder of one of his mechanics, Alanso. He flexed his fingers around the torque wrench he'd retrieved for the man, refusing to let go and trace the path perspiration took over deceptively wiry muscles.

Inked artwork brightened as the bead dampened several tattoos. First a tribal scribble, then a portrait of Al's long-lost mom, and finally the top of an intricate cross that disappeared beneath the bunched fabric clinging around his waist. Torn and oil-stained coveralls hugged a high, tight ass.

All Eli could think of these days was that goddamned ass, which Alanso now shoved out in his direction while the bastard tuned some rich kid's engine. With hardly any effort at all, Eli could smack it. Or bite it. Or fuck it.

Son of a bitch.

Nothing good could come of this obsession. Damn his cousin Joe for putting crazy thoughts in his brain. The guy was a member of a construction crew that liked to work hard and play harder together. Their polyamorous bedroom gymnastics had become obvious when Eli and Alanso had walked in on a scene he couldn't forget. But just because that bastard had been lucky enough to find a whole team of fuck buddies his wife adored—no, loved—didn't mean such a wild arrangement could work for everybody in the world.

Eli had no right to wish for the same. Yet lately, each time he looked at the half dozen guys and girl he considered his grease monkey family, he found himself sporting a hard-on stiff enough to jack up a tank with. Thankfully, the oblivious gang hadn't identified the source of his recent frustration. Though they certainly had borne the brunt of his bad temper, adding guilt to the unslakable arousal stripping his gears, leaving him spinning his wheels.

Stuck and stranded. Alone with his dirty little secret.

Except for Alanso.

Why had that mechanic been the one to witness Joe and his crew's alternative loving along with Eli? Probably because they went most everywhere together. Eli shoved the memory of his right-hand man's right hand from his mind. Or at least he tried. The guy had tortured Eli's cock with greedy pumps of his trembling fist while the crew's foreman, Mike, demonstrated just how hot it could be to take on one of his own. By fucking Joe while the mechanics had stared, in awe of the power exchange.

Grunts had spilled from Joe's mouth, which knocked against his wife's breast as he took everything Mike gave him then begged for more. The audible decadence echoed through Eli's mind day in and day out. In perfect harmony with the memory of Alanso's answering cries as he witnessed the undeniable claiming.

Eli knew that if he slammed Alanso against the 426 inch engine block of that 1970 Dodge Challenger R/T coupe, the man would spread and welcome him.

Boss, friend...brother.

And that's where the fantasy turned to battery acid, burning Eli's insides with the bitter taste of responsibility and logic.

How could he want a guy he considered family? How could he violate that trust?

He couldn't afford to lose Alanso.

Not from his business, definitely not from his life.

So he could never seize what he craved. Frustration bubbled over.

"What's taking so long, Diaz?" Eli knocked thick, bunched biceps with the tool he carried. "We're trying to make a profit here, you know?"

Alanso couldn't seem to wipe his glare away as easily as he rid his brow of the moisture dotting it. He snatched the wrench from Eli and returned to his task without taking the bait. If Eli couldn't fuck, the least the guy could do was give him the courtesy of engaging in a decent fight. His teeth ground together.

"You hear me, *huevón*? This isn't some charity case. Hot Rods is a business. Don't spend all day on a five-hundred-dollar job." Eli thumped the hood, knowing how the impact would reverberate.

Alanso's shoulders tensed. The clench of muscles along his spine altered the shape of his tattoos. Still, he said nothing about the low blow—or how he'd repaid the Londons a million times over for their hand-up through a solid decade of friendship and loyalty—and continued about his job. One he was damn fine at performing. No one could make an engine purr like Alanso.

"You want half-assed, go hire a motorman from the chain in town." He didn't bother to acknowledge Eli with a look.

Still, as Alanso's boss and best friend, Eli knew that tone well enough. It'd be accompanied by Al's tattooed middle finger sticking up along that wrench, he'd bet.

The defiance made Eli long to grab the other man's chin and force him to gaze up. Maybe then Alanso would see the desperation making Eli more unhinged than Mustang Sally during a particularly bad bout of PMS. God help them all.

He'd never wanted something he couldn't have so badly before. Except maybe to heal his mom during those horrid weeks she'd spent dying.

Terror and a soul-deep pain that never entirely faded turned him into something no better than a cornered animal. Eli lashed out. "Good idea. Maybe they'd spend less time checking me out and do their goddamned work."

A *clang* surprised him. He didn't quite realize what had happened until a spark flew from the metal tool where it connected with the concrete floor of the garage. Alanso had winged the thing an inch or less from Eli's thankfully steel-toed boot when he spun around.

He wouldn't have missed by accident.

"*Para el carajo!* Maybe I should've done more than look. You're obviously too

5

hardheaded to man up and come for me. So the deal's off the table. I've wasted too much time on a dude who's in denial. You're right about that." Alanso sneered. "I'm tired of waiting for you to grow some *cojones*."

"Keep your voice down." Eli checked over his shoulder. Kaige and Carver didn't so much as glance in their direction, but the stillness of their bodies made it clear they caught at least wisps of the conversation. Years of tough living had taught the men to tread lightly in conflict. At least until swinging a punch became necessary. Then it was likely to become a free-for-all.

"*Joder! Now* you want to shut me up. *Come mierda*." Alanso scrubbed a hand over his bald head, leaving a streak of oil that tempted Eli to buff it away, maybe with his five o'clock shadow. "Wouldn't want the rest of the Hot Rods hearing about the good life and how we're not living it, right? They might revolt."

"Hey, I've never kept anyone against their will. You all chose to stay here. With me. The door's open." Eli waved toward the enormous rolling metal sheets that protected the garage bays at night or when the weather turned cold. Through them, the pumps of the service station his dad had started were visible.

A flash of something miserable twisted Alanso's usually smiling lips into a grimace.

The gesture had Eli thinking of something other than what it would feel like to get a blowjob from the man. That was a first after weeks of studying that mouth.

He reached out, but it was too late. Alanso dodged, taking a step back and then another.

"You know what, Cobra." He grabbed his crotch hard enough to make Eli wince. "You can suck it. Or, then again... No, you can't. That fucking checkered flag has dropped, *amigo*."

Reflex, instinct, dread—something— inspired Eli to lunge for the man who turned away. Warm, moist skin met his palm.

"Get your fucking hands off me." When the engine guru pivoted, the unusual chill in his brown eyes froze Eli in his tracks. "You had your chance. You blew it. For us both. I'm out of here."

"You're quitting?" Eli gaped as the bottom fell out of his stomach. "Wait—"

"Hell no. I told you I'm over that bus-stop phase." Alanso sliced his hand through the air between them. His knuckles skimmed Eli's chest. They left a slash of fire across his heart. "I've got places to go and people to do. There are things I gotta learn about myself. And for the first time since we were fifteen, you're not going to be a part of that with me. Your loss."

"Shit. I-I'm sorry." Eli couldn't find a way to say what for. For violating their friendship, for wanting to destroy what they had or for acting like an ass by postponing the inevitable—he couldn't make up his mind. "Don't go."

They'd drawn a crowd. Even Roman inched closer now. The tough yet quiet guy stared openly at their spectacle. Charged air had somehow tipped off Sally too. She emerged from the painting booth, crossing the bays at an alarming rate. If she got tangled up in this, Eli would never forgive himself. Of all their gang, he knew better than to trample on her emotions. Her heart would rip in two if she had any idea of the rift opening at his feet right now.

Just like his chest was hewn.

"I'm not *leaving* leaving, Cobra." Alanso lowered his voice. "This is my home. I hope some things haven't changed. Let me know if I'm no longer welcome and I'll pack my shit. But I can't fucking do this anymore. Not for another damn minute. I have to know what it's like. To be honest about who I am and what I want. Before I lose any more respect for either of us."

"Fine then." Eli leaned forward before he could stop himself. The awful sensations sliding through his guts had to stop. Fast.

Before the rest of the garage got caught in their crossfire. He shoved Alanso hard enough the man stumbled across the threshold before catching his balance. It felt like forcing a baby bird from the nest. He only hoped Al spread his wings fast enough. "Get the hell out. Do what you gotta do."

Alanso mouthed a plea out of sight of the guys now wiping hands on coveralls and milling near in a semi-circle. "Come with me."

Eli slammed his fist on the big red button on the doorframe beside him. With an ominous rattle, the metal door began to lower between them, severing all communication as completely as if the aluminum were a drawbridge over a monster-filled moat.

The scream of a crotch rocket taking off at an unwise speed ricocheted through their space. Gravel *pinged* when it slung against the barrier he'd erected.

"What the fuck did you do to him, Cobra?" Sally canted her head as she laid into Eli. "You've really been acting like a snake lately, ever since Dave's accident. Hissing at anyone who comes near. We get that you're afraid of losing people important to you. The crew's near miss seems to have scared you stupid. I get it, I do."

He closed his eyes, trying to block out the concern she voiced for all the rest of the guys staring at him.

"But keep going like you are and you'll drive him away."

"Stop talking, *Salome*." He knew better than to tell her to shut up, even if she didn't understand how her insight cut him. Hopefully using her full name would be enough to convey how serious he was. He couldn't dive into the details.

No way could he admit what he and Alanso had seen. What they'd done.

"You better not have let your fear hurt him. Tell me you didn't." Her emerald eyes begged much more softly than her steely tone.

Eli didn't bother to lie.

The hand she let fly didn't catch him by surprise. She loved Alanso. They all did.

Which was why he didn't bother to duck. He deserved the stinging impact of her open palm on his cheek. That and more. Because even as his head whipped to the side, he admired the stretch of her petite frame when she stood on her tiptoes, her raven hair and the glint of her fancy-painted fingernails, one of her pride and joys.

If he'd only wanted Alanso, maybe the two of them could have explored the possibility.

But he was going to hell because he lusted after all of the Hot Rods.

The gang held their collective breath, waiting to see how he would react to Sally's uncharacteristic act of violence. Roman stiffened, prepared to spring to her defense.

All the fight leeched out of Eli.

No matter how bad it got, they didn't have to be afraid he'd attack one of their own. Then again, hadn't he done just that?

The damage he'd wrought would be far worse than the impact of a fist.

His shoulders dropped and his head hung. "I'll get him back."

"You'd fucking better." Mustang Sally shook her hand before propping it on her hip and pointing to the door. "Don't come home without him."

The five remaining guys closed rank around their littlest member. They knew she'd hate for Eli to see her tears or her alarm. He didn't waste any time offering comfort she wouldn't welcome. Kaige, Carver, Holden, Roman and Bryce would take good care of her.

They didn't need him.

But Alanso might.

CHAPTER TWO

Eli punched one of the three metal supports on his Shelby Cobra's steering wheel. The solid construction of the original part ensured it wouldn't bend beneath his punishment. It hurt the hell out of his knuckles, though. Pain obscured some of the alarm bubbling through his gut.

This was the last of the bars in a twenty-mile radius of the Hot Rods garage. Alanso's current crotch rocket—a Honda REPSOL 600RR with a ridiculous #69 racing decal—was nowhere in sight. The neon orange body and wheels would have been impossible to miss, even at night.

He'd hoped to sit shoulder to shoulder with his best friend and drown their sorrows together. Then they could have called Sally to pick them up and things would have been back to normal by the time they commiserated over their killer hangovers in the morning.

Wasn't much a bottle of Southern Comfort mixed with a few drops of cola couldn't fix. At least, that's how they'd gotten through most of life's disappointments in the past.

Well, once they'd been old enough. Or bold enough to sneak some of Roman's stash. The guy was four years older than Eli and had a couple more on Alanso. They'd roped him into the group when he'd been twenty-going-on-forty. He'd spent so much time wasted he'd never seemed to mind picking them up an extra bottle from the liquor store.

Eli's dad, Tom London, had reined in Roman and the rest of the Hot Rods, never letting their habits get them in too much trouble. He'd walked a fine line, mentoring the damaged kids while allowing them to make their own mistakes. Somehow he'd managed to keep from scaring them away from the safe haven he'd created as a legacy to his late wife, despite his own often-crippling agony.

Hell, more than once Tom had decided if he couldn't beat 'em, he should join 'em and put down his fair share of liquid fire, bonding them closer with every drink. It might not have been a recommended approach by *Parenting* magazine, but it worked for them.

And now Eli had jeopardized one of their own.

He squeezed the chrome knob on top of his shifter, out of ideas. All but one.

It was a long shot, but he had nowhere else to turn.

Parking at the far edge of the lot, away from people or other cars, he withdrew his phone from the pocket of his jeans. To extricate the device he had to lift up slightly in the leather bucket seat of his restored Shelby Cobra. Damn Salome and her fashion advice. Hot or not, these jeans didn't leave a lot of room to maneuver. Plus, he felt like he might display some coin slot when he bent over in the low-rise denim. Being a typical mechanic didn't suit his style.

He cursed as he wriggled.

By the time he swiped open his contact list, he grimaced. Confessing his stupidity wouldn't be easy. He gritted his teeth and poked the icon of his cousin Joe smiling like a lunatic next to his gorgeous wife, who cradled their son.

The picture was a few months old. Eli took a second to wonder at how much the little guy had grown in even that short period of time. Like a weed, and bulkier every day. Hopefully the kid liked football. It'd be a shame to waste a build like that. They had a pretty good idea of how gargantuan he'd turn out to be.

After all, their friend Dave was the largest of Joe's crewmates. Considering baby Nathan's dove gray eyes and the shade of his dark hair—which exactly matched his honorary uncle's mop—it was pretty clear who'd contributed the winning swimmer to the crew's effort to give Morgan a baby when Joe hadn't been able.

The crew had survived some serious issues, navigating tricky waters. Nothing had been handed to them on a silver platter. Maybe Eli should pull his head out of his ass and quit moping long enough to formulate a roadmap to his dream destination.

Lost in thought, it wasn't until the third ring that Eli considered the time. *Fuck!*

They'd been working the later hours their customers loved when Alanso had split. It had to be... A glance at his watch confirmed—after eleven o'clock. Add another hour for the time difference and he winced.

About to hang up, Eli jumped when Joe's voice came across the line.

"Hey." His cousin's answer sounded a little gruff.

In the background, a baby cried.

"Oh shit, sorry." Eli let his head fall back against the leather rest. "I didn't think about how late it is. Did I wake Nathan up?"

"Nah. He's being fussy tonight. The last few days, actually." Joe groaned. "It's not like him. He's usually so quiet, perfect. It's making Morgan nervous that he's not feeling well. Kay and Dave are here too, calming us down. Or trying, at least. Their theory is Nathan's getting his first tooth. Dave said his little sisters got theirs around six months too."

"Ah, damn. I'm sorry to hear that." Eli ran his hand through his short hair. "I'll let you get back to your family, then."

"Honestly, I'll give you ten bucks if you don't." Joe sighed. "I need a minute to myself. Besides, you *are* family."

"If you're sure—"

"Don't make me beg, asshole." His cousin raised his voice a bit. "Hey guys, it's Eli. I'm going to step out on the landing for a few."

"King Cobra!" Dave rumbled a hello while two feminine greetings mingled in the background. "Hey Nathmeister, tell Uncle Eli his truck's running great."

"Of course it is. We don't build shit at Hot Rods." And Alanso had personally attended to every detail of the project after *that* night. The night they'd seen how badly Dave's injury impacted the rest of his crew. The night they'd watched the guys and their female soul mates comfort each other in their friend's absence.

"Are you going to pay his speeding tickets too, Cobra?" Kayla sounded half-annoyed, but even the chastisement couldn't hide her affection for her husband. Not since a freak accident had nearly stolen him from her.

"I can't be held responsible for his actions. Though I heartily approve." His soul lightened in seconds. *Tough times are temporary.* That's what he'd always told himself and the rest of the Hot Rods when someone had a bad night.

"All right, Eli. I'm heading outside." The ambient sounds got less amplified. "You're off speaker. What's up?"

"Maybe I called to see how you're doing." It didn't seem fair to add to Joe's burdens.

"Eh, we'll be fine. It's just the joys of parenthood. Thank God for the crew. I don't know how Mo and I would do this alone. We're spoiled, I know. Stronger together in the group. But even still it's a lot sometimes." Joe paused. "It's a ton of responsibility to care for another person. An innocent. Seeing Kate and Mike going through the same helps some. Hell, Mike carries all of us on his shoulders sometimes, like you do for your gang. But every once in a while I have to take a step back or I'll drive myself nuts, you know?"

"Of course. You worry so much because you love them." Eli was suddenly glad he'd reached out tonight. He should do it more often. For both their sakes. Why couldn't the crew live closer? "If you didn't you wouldn't deserve them. We both know the world isn't always perfect. Shitty things happen to good people. Look at Dave."

"And your mom," Joe's voice was low, but it carried across the two states between them.

"Yeah." Eli silently added Alanso to that list as well. He had to make this right.

"When I think back on that summer—" Joe didn't need to spell out which one. Eli would remember it for the rest of his life. In grotesque detail. "It's still not quite real to me. Sort of like a movie. I can see myself, you, your dad. Like zombies. Staggering around, trying to figure out how to make it to the next day and the next. And then the shit with Dave last year... Well, it made me not want to fuck around ever. I tell my family, all of them, how much I love them. Every day. I'm terrified of losing them."

"I hear you. The ache never goes away." Eli rubbed his chest. "But what can you do? Lock yourself out of life to spare yourself the pain?"

"Personally, I wouldn't advocate that plan, no." His cousin bit the statement off.

"Am I missing something here? We're talking about you, right?" Narrowing his eyes, Eli stared into the darkness.

19

"Not anymore." A sardonic chuckle rang across the airwaves. "You do realize Alanso's been videochatting with us a lot—almost every night for the past month now, right? Hell, I think him and James talk more than a couple of teenage girls."

"What?" Eli sat up straighter. "Why?"

"I'd assume because his best fucking friend is making him uncomfortable with sharing too much. Or maybe refuses to discuss certain issues at all. Probably because the one guy he should be able to trust with his insecurities and hopes seems to have forgotten that not everyone gets a tomorrow. And there's no going back."

"Son of a bitch!" Eli's heart pounded as he took the lashing from his cousin. Sickness washed over him as he recalled the last time he'd seen his mother. Surrounded by flowers from the uncounted people she'd helped in her social work, she'd cautioned him to always lead with his heart before slipping peacefully from the world.

Would she respect him for keeping his hands off the guy he was closer to than a brother? Or would she shake her head at his callous treatment of another human being? Deep down, he knew the answer. Failing her shredded his insides.

"Even Kate said she's disappointed in you, Cobra." Refusing to pull his punches, Joe let him have it. "Are you that fucking scared?"

First Sally, now Joe. Screw them. "I'm not—"

"Yeah, you are." A snarl from the usually laidback man surprised Eli. When Joe broke their mutual silence, he spoke with a hell of a lot more kindness. Eli might have preferred poison to the pity he sensed now. "You don't have to lie to me. I was there. I know what it did to you when your mom died. But I'm telling you now, you're making a mistake. If you don't fix this, you'll be saying goodbye to Alanso too."

"Fine. I hear you." The phone trembled in his hold. "I just don't see how this can work. If I fuck it up, he'll leave. We won't have even what we do now. How can I take that chance?"

"He can't settle for friends without lying to himself. Hell, to you both. Don't make him do that. He won't last. Neither of you will."

"But Joe…"

"What, E?"

A deep breath delayed his response. "It's not just Alanso. I want what you have. Fucker."

Joe laughed. "I don't blame you. And I think you've got a shot. I remember those stories you told about the wild nights some of the guys have had. They're open to unconventional. Plus, you know your Hot Rods. Deep in your gut, you understand what they need. I can't imagine how your pasts affect you individually, let alone together, but I gotta think you wouldn't have stuck together so long if you didn't rely on that bond to make it through."

"Yeah, the Island of Misfit Mechanics. That's us. So how the fuck do I deal with seven guys and one chick in some crazy-ass relationship? I've never even had a steady girlfriend for Christ's sake." He might grow his hair longer just so he could pull it out. He had a feeling he might find the option handy in the coming months.

"I'd recommend starting slow. Walk before you run and all that shit. Go get Alanso out of that hellhole. Make things right with him. In the crew, it all began with Neil and James. They showed us what we were missing. It didn't take long to catch on, though. Start the fire, Eli. Let it burn."

"Wait." Hope rose in his soul. "You know where Alanso is?"

"I might." Joe laughed. "Depending on if you're going to keep being a toolbox or not."

"You said 'hellhole'." No more kidding for Eli. "Is he in trouble? Damn it! Don't fuck around if he is."

"Nothing he can't handle...probably." A hint of unease colored Joe's statement. "Promise you won't march in there and drag him out just because you think it's the right thing for him. He didn't make this decision lightly. You have to support him. As long as he's not being hurt, you can't get your tighty-whiteys all in a bunch over his little experiment after you refused to play along."

"You mean there's a chance he *is* being hurt?" Eli pinched the bridge of his nose. "What the fuck, Joe? You know I'd do anything for my guys. And Mustang Sally. Tell me where he is. I'll go to him. I'll...try."

"About the best we could hope for, I suppose." A door shutting was followed by Nathan's sobs. They'd slowed and muted but hadn't disappeared entirely. Eli could relate. "Mo, what's the name of the park I wrote down over there?"

A *park*? What the fuck—?

"Chestnut Grove." Eli didn't hesitate. He fired up the engine with a flick of his wrist and slammed the shifter into reverse. "He went to a pick-up spot? Sex with strangers? Jesus."

Morgan echoed the name, confirming his fears.

"Go gentle on him." Kayla called in the background. "He needs you."

23

"You've got this, King Cobra." Dave added his support.

"We love you," Morgan called.

"And so does Alanso," Joe added. "Don't let him down tonight."

"It's going to take me at least twenty minutes to get there. He left hours ago. What if I'm too late? What if someone's taking advantage of him?" Eli fishtailed as he zipped onto the road and gunned it.

"More likely he's having a helluva good time." The smile coloring Joe's tone faded a bit. "But just in case, maybe you'd better drive it like you stole it."

"I got that." Eli short-shifted into fourth and pressed the pedal to the floor. His Cobra cornered like a champ on the new suspension Kaige had installed last week.

"Right. So time to hang up. Keep calm, lead with your heart and have fun." Joe's smile rang through his tone. "Call us when you can, so we know you're both all right and we can say we told you so."

"Hey, Joe." His cousin surely expected an insult. "In case this is *my* last day…I love you too. Thanks."

He disconnected the call, tossed his phone onto the passenger seat and watched the speedometer climb.

CHAPTER THREE

"**Y**ou like what you see?"

Alanso checked over his shoulder to confirm the older Latino dude wearing lots of chains had actually intended for him to answer. He thought he'd lurked far enough in the shadows to escape notice.

Maybe he'd made a sound when a couple of the younger guys milling around had approached, scuffling for the honor of kneeling at the man's feet. Each guy offered his mouth to give the bear one hell of a lube job.

Gracious, the guy welcomed them both. With a hand on each of their heads, he drew them closer to his crotch even as he smiled at Alanso.

"Yeah. I'm talking to you, baldy." His laugh held a bit of an edge. "You know it's pitchblack out here. You can lose the pretty sunglasses. Unless you're famous and wandered into 'Nut Grove by accident. Afraid people'll recognize you?"

Alanso shook his head.

"You aren't married, are you? I don't screw around on people's promises. You'll find some here that do if that's your thing. Somebody for everybody pretty much. Not us, though."

"Nah. Nothing like that." Alanso peeled his shades off and tucked one of the arms into the V of his white T-shirt. He liked the way his tattoos showed through the thin cotton. Each inked symbol helped keep him focused on a life motto, lent him strength or illustrated a badge of courage he'd earned.

He rubbed his thumb back and forth over the *R* on his right index finger—part of the Hot Rods label he'd indelibly inscribed on his body. A car drove across his left pinky followed by one letter on each finger, a permanent reminder of the group that had imprinted themselves on his soul.

Tonight, for the first time in over a decade, he embarked on a journey without one of his garagemates. He frowned and rubbed the marking faster.

He'd survived some rough times before stumbling across Eli and his dad at the youth center. As a child he'd drifted from couch to couch owned by gracious members of his

Cuban-American extended family until he realized how he burdened families with enough mouths of their own to feed. After that, he'd survived on the streets in gangs of transient teens—most of them orphaned by deported parents—not so different from himself. Except that crime didn't appeal to him as a profession.

Still, he hadn't had to watch his own back in long enough that he felt soft. But he could hold his own. The knife in his pocket was a last resort kind of insurance. His brawling skills would probably render the precaution unnecessary.

"Quit biting that lip and get your sexy *culo* over here. Phil and Ronnie will make room for you, won't you, boys?" The top knocked his boot into the sides of their knees, urging them apart.

The guys must have liked the way the ringleader's cock tasted because they didn't stop licking it long enough to complain about sharing the adequate, but not overly impressive, hard-on. Alanso imagined they were as desperate as he was, waiting for their bimonthly clandestine fix.

He'd heard rumors about this place and the things that happened on a random night every couple of weeks. Luck had been in his favor when he'd overheard some guys passing the news of the next date while he'd used a bar bathroom a few days ago. Adrenaline had run rampant through his system since. Could he go through with a visit?

Excitement and a little bit of terror had left him no choice but to check it out. He worried this could become a habit.

He had every kind of intimacy with the Hot Rods he could want—love, laughter, shared pain, pride in their workmanship. All but one. Sexual. He couldn't do without that final gear anymore. Riding shotgun while they stalked women had quit being fun when he admitted to himself that none of the garage bunnies who threw themselves at Middletown's infamous bad boys stacked up to Sally. And that was even before his eyes had opened to other possibilities.

Hopeless ones.

King Cobra would never let him risk their friendship—his and Eli's, their and Sally's or the various combinations of the larger group—on a romp. Despite the fact that some of the guys had teamed up before, it'd always been a fling, nothing serious. Definitely not a relationship like the crew had built. That was risky. If something went wrong it could tear them apart. So he stalled.

As much as Alanso wanted both Eli and Sally, he couldn't stop dreaming about the complex polyamorous relationship he'd witnessed thriving in the crew. And if he couldn't have that unbound wild love with his gang, he at least had to know if his recent distaste for a night of no-strings fucking had to do with the gender of his mattress buddies.

So why couldn't he force his boots to unglue from the matted grass?

"I'm not sure sharing is my thing." *Liar!* His brain shouted at him, knowing full well that if the trio on display before him were Cobra, Kaige and Bryce—or any other combination of Hot Rods—he'd skid across the mostly cleared area beneath the makeshift pavilion like a World Series player stealing home.

"Trying to play it cool, are you?" The man jerked his chin in Alanso's direction. "I can spot that bulge from here, even in this shitty light. Impressive for a Mexican."

"*Pendejo*, I'm Cuban." Alanso tried to keep from letting this fucker get his hackles up. That wasn't the part of either of them he cared to rouse tonight.

"No kidding." The guy rolled his eyes. "Your accent is pretty distinct. My grandmother's from Matanzas. But I did get you to come closer, didn't I?"

"I don't have an accent." He tipped his head.

One of the guys—Ronnie, he thought—still sucking away, choked, as if on a laugh.

Alanso glared at him.

"Hey now. We're an equal opportunity kind of gathering here." The guy smiled a bit, his face starting to relax as the men teasing him proved they were good at what they did. Maybe they'd teach Alanso a thing or two. "Come on, kid. I'm not going to last forever. Take what you want. At least let me get a better look at you while I cream their faces."

The top grunted. The guys at his feet braced his thighs.

Alanso swallowed hard and glanced away.

White Christmas lights decorated the stand of trees that sheltered like-minded men who had nowhere else to turn for what they needed. It was almost romantic and utterly heartbreaking simultaneously. He wished his first intentional male-on-male experience could have happened somewhere he felt more comfortable.

Like maybe Eli's desk in the garage office or up against a stack of tires.

He didn't count the day he'd actually touched the person he wanted most. Okay, fine, *one* of the people. Damn Joe and the crew for poisoning his brain with dirty possibilities. They'd guaranteed he was unsatisfied with anything short of a tender gangbang.

Meanwhile, Eli had obviously been too shocked to listen to his better fucking judgment in the heat of the moment, but he'd snapped into shape as soon as they'd hit the highway toward home. Refusing to talk about what'd happened, he had slammed the door on any relapses.

At least Alanso had experienced heaven once. The memory of Eli's moans—and the heat of his come pouring over the Hot Rods tattoos on Alanso's knuckles—would fill his mind as he fooled around with another man tonight. His imagination was strong enough to superimpose the crucial details over his make-do experience.

Vivid enough they'd drive him to ecstasy or at least action.

Going home without having taken his bisexuality for a test drive was not an option. Sure, he liked fooling around with women plenty. But now that he admitted to himself he'd always been kind of curious about men, he felt like he'd starved that part of him for far too long. The pussy he'd scored since the eye-opening round with the crew just hadn't satisfied him.

The urge to fuck—to be fucked—had grown in him until it hurt.

And Eli hadn't been there to take away the ache this time.

No more.

But he could use some help getting started. He hadn't dared stop for a fortifying drink. Not when he was riding his motorcycle, and definitely not when he was flying solo over new territory. "Look, I—uh, I've *mostly* never done this before."

"Sure you haven't." The guy snorted. "It's been my first time every other week for the last decade too."

So long in a meaningless cycle. Why hadn't this guy found a lover? One he could take in the light of day? Was Alanso doomed to hiding in the shadows if he did this tonight? No, it was just a trial. A way to find out what he really wanted before he gambled with bigger stakes.

"I thought I could watch this time around." And if it got him hot enough, maybe he'd do a little taste testing of his own.

"Sorry, kid. That's not how it works. No play, no stay." The veteran shrugged somewhat apologetically. "Otherwise, how do we know you're not going to narc on us? Or take incriminating pictures or some shit? Get dirty like we do or go back to momma."

"That *puta* left me behind years ago." He slipped his fingers through his belt loops to keep from stroking the tattoo of her on his shoulder. "Kicked out of the country. Sent back to Havana. Couldn't be bothered to lug a brat with her."

Why the hell was he telling a stranger that?

One of the cuties, Phil, manipulating the standing guy paused. He pressed a kiss to the side of the ultra-stiff shaft in his fist and peeked up at Alanso. "No one's rejecting you tonight. Come over here."

Alanso clenched his jaw and nodded once. "Maybe."

The second man on his knees lifted his head and winked up at the guy he serviced. "He's cute. Can we keep the new guy, Links?"

"It's up to him." Links held out his hand as his playthings adjusted their places. Chains rattled as they brushed against his cargo pants. "You want to play with us, *cariño*?"

"I think I do. Yeah." Alanso scrunched his eyes closed a moment before stepping forward. He hadn't realized he'd crossed the space until one of the men pressed his palms to Alanso's thighs.

"We'll go easy on you." He nuzzled the crotch of Alanso's jeans. The deep breath Ronnie drew made him self-conscious for not making a pit stop at the apartment above Hot Rods, which he shared with the rest of his garagemates, to change before heading out. Had he hesitated, even for a moment, he wouldn't have been able to go through with this. As it was, he'd driven around for hours before pointing his bike in this direction.

"I'm pretty sure I'd prefer it if you didn't." He held out his hand, feeling ridiculous. "I'm Al."

"A pleasure." Phil smiled while Ronnie growled and tugged the waist of Alanso's jeans.

"Help us with Links. Or get your peeking in while we work. I'm suddenly hungry for dessert."

Alanso allowed his knees to collapse. A puff of dirt rose around him. His shoulders bumped into the guys now flanking him. The heat they radiated was welcome.

"Ain't that a pretty sight?" Links thrust his hips forward, rubbing his cock over Phil's cheek before presenting his tool to Alanso. "Go ahead. Try it. You might like it."

"That's what I'm afraid of." He looked inward, measured the pulse of excitement flooding his veins and decided this was it.

Time to find out once and for all.

"One thing...I'm doing this the safe way or not at all." Alanso wouldn't budge on that requirement. If he ever did get another shot with Eli, or Sally, or any of the other guys, he refused to put them in danger.

"Damn, I'd like to be in your mouth bare. But I get you don't know us. Yet." Links dug in his pocket and withdrew a couple of condoms. "Mint or cherry?"

"Go for the mint," Phil advised. "It's like brushing your teeth. Covers up the rubber taste."

He nodded.

Links ripped the foil and sheathed himself so fast Alanso figured he'd done it a million times before. The guys beside him each wrapped an arm around his waist, drawing him into their fold. They helped him lean forward despite the pebbles gouging his knees. Links brushed the pad of his thumb over Alanso's lips, triggering his reflexive opening.

The three men fed him his first taste of male flesh.

His eyes went wide, and his gaze locked on Links'.

"Mmm, you like that? Yeah. I knew you would." The guy splayed his fingers on Alanso's bald head and rubbed the shiny surface of his scalp.

Alanso weighed the plump, if not huge, cock on his tongue. He suckled lightly, then a bit harder. It felt nice in his mouth. Warm, firm and full. His eyes drifted closed as he went for another nibble.

"You're fucking hot. A waste to never have had this mouth fucked before."

The guy was getting into it now. Really.

"Enjoy while you can, Al," Ronnie cheered him on. "Links is close already. We got him good and riled for you. Maybe next time you'll taste him. A little sweaty, a little salty."

"Shit, Phil." Ronnie ground against Alanso's left side, prodding his hip with a thick shaft encased in denim. "Cut that out or you're going to make me come in my pants again."

"I have a feeling we'll both be up for more than one round after this." He smiled at his friend.

"Probably true." The guy practically vibrated where they fused together.

Alanso could relate. His tongue lapped along the coated underside of Links' erection, making him half-freak-out and half-celebrate. He was doing it. Really doing it. And *coño*, it felt good. Right.

Almost perfect.

Alanso relaxed his jaw, permitting himself to take Links farther into his mouth. He didn't stop until the head of the guy's cock stabbed the back of his throat and he choked. The men on either side of him pulled him off.

"Don't get all crazy now, Al." Phil rubbed his shoulders. "You'll have plenty of chances to practice if you want them. Go slow tonight. Enjoy this."

He moaned. The vibration had Links' cock jerking on the tip of his tongue. He craned his neck and sucked harder.

"Careful. Teeth," the guy panted.

Alanso thought of all the sloppy BJs he'd had from too-drunk chicks and tried to focus. When he did, he swirled his tongue around the ridges made by the veins now standing out on Links' shaft. He worked up the length, learning the textures and shapes along the way until he got to the plump head.

Alanso closed his lips around the tip of Links' cock and suckled. He flicked his tongue through the indentation made by the slit at the top, smearing superslick precome from the divot onto the reservoir of the condom. A shiver ran down his spine as he imagined the bulge filling with seed.

"Goddamn," Links growled.

"He's a natural." Phil patted Alanso's ass.

"Go ahead. Take him deeper. Slow this time," Ronnie coached him. "Be ready. You probably won't get far before he goes off."

The four men braced each other in a ring, each of them fully engaged in the moment.

Alanso felt part of something...bigger...than his simple arousal.

What if it were Carver, Holden and Eli sharing the moment with him? Sally and Roman? Bryce? Kaige? Something this powerful would forge an unbreakable bond. He'd never have to worry about losing them again. Not like his mom.

Desperation forced him to suck harder than intended. He sealed Links' fate.

"Oh shit, yeah." The man's fingers dug into Alanso's shoulders. The tiny pain was welcome.

"Keep going," Phil encouraged. "Drain him dry."

His throat flexed as Links shouted and squirmed. The minty cock in his mouth swelled then jerked as Alanso's first satisfied customer filled his condom with a thick load. For Alanso. He'd pleased a man. An experienced, kind of jaded guy.

Phil tapped his chin. "Okay, Al. Let him go. He's spent."

He opened his mouth. A whimper escaped along with limp flesh when Links' cock slipped free. Alanso's hand flew to his jeans and ripped them open before jamming his fist inside.

"Oh hell no." Ronnie tugged his wrist.

Alanso nearly decked the man. He could come with a few good jerks.

Links hit the dirt on his knees just as Phil and his partner colluded to shove Alanso backward. He fell to the ground, his shoulders slamming into the clearing. For one tiny second, fear shriveled his balls.

"Shh. Nothing to fight here, Al." Phil held him down gently. Alanso could have broken the hold at any time. "Let us take care of you like you deserve."

"Me?" He hadn't considered that.

"Yeah." Phil grinned, a wolf's smile. "It's your turn."

CHAPTER FOUR

Eli balled his fists to keep from charging into the clearing and taking a swing at the men who dared to put their hands on his best friend. But Joe's warning rang in his mind. He had no right to interfere. He'd rejected Alanso's advances. Given up the chance to be the man reveling in the seduction of Al's innocent mouth on his cock.

What a fucking moron.

Except he wouldn't have worn some nasty fucking condom. Alanso knew where he'd been. Hell, they'd been there together most of the time.

Jealousy burned through him, nearly as hot and bright as desire.

About the time Alanso really got into his amazing-looking blowjob, Eli unknitted his zipper and withdrew his cock. He took himself in hand, stroking in time to the uneven lunges of Alanso's mouth on the guy they'd called Links' shaft. The flex and play of muscles around the edges of Alanso's T-shirt only fired him up more.

Eli wished he could feel the strength there as Alanso submitted to him. Not because he had some sick urge to lord over the guy. But because he had waited so long for Alanso to trust that his friends would always care for him, wounded or not. Once and for all, maybe he'd believe that none of his friends would ever choose to leave him behind.

Yet, in some ways, wasn't that exactly what he'd done by refusing to walk beside his best friend on this journey?

His cock wilted for a split second until Alanso's science project lost his control. The man broke, grabbing Al's head and anchoring him in place as he rode the open, succulent mouth in front of him and shot his come into the condom in spasm after spasm of what looked like a world-class orgasm.

Eli half-expected the guy to drop dead on the spot.

He wanted to hate the bastard. But he was thankful that Links had given Alanso what he needed when Eli couldn't. That the stranger had respected Al, taking pleasure while giving plenty in return. Fuck them.

All three of the apparent regulars now hovered around Alanso. His cheeks were darker than usual, a flush on his tan skin, and his chest rose and fell rapidly. The nice one, Phil, petted Alanso as if he were a stray dog to be tamed. Meanwhile, his accomplice shimmied those hot-as-hell jeans then a pair of bright yellow-and-black boxer briefs over Al's trim hips and down his powerful thighs.

Eli leaned against a tree so he wouldn't crash to the forest floor at the sight of Alanso's dick, rock-hard. Sure, they'd shaken the ketchup bottle together plenty of times as teenagers. All of the Hot Rods except Sally had whipped it out periodically during those hormone-laden years when Roman would bring home a porno or one of the other guys had gotten lucky in the storeroom of the garage.

But he swore he didn't remember Alanso's cock looking like that.

It shamed Eli that he hadn't noticed the heft and impressive girth of Alanso's hard-on when he'd clasped it in his fist the day they'd discovered just how close the crew really was. To be honest, he'd been too mesmerized by Mike fucking Joe and overwhelmed by the possibilities to take it all in.

Plus, if he'd allowed himself to concentrate on Alanso's cock spewing all over his hand, he never could have returned to normal once they'd left the fantasyland of their mutual masturbation and returned to the garage. *Fuck*. Had he gotten this entirely wrong from the start?

Maybe he should have done exactly the opposite.

Months and months of torture could have been alleviated for them both.

Because Eli knew as he watched the three men in the grove undress Alanso—slowly yet deliberately—that he would have to do the same someday before he died. Or he'd regret it with every breath he took.

Bronze skin coated in a light sheen of perspiration glinted in the twinkling lights wrapped through the bushes. Alanso looked like a sacrifice staked out on the turf. Or maybe a god surrounded by devotees.

Eli could understand.

He leaned forward as Phil dropped down to tease Alanso's beaded nipple and the stainless steel barbell running through it. Eli had imagined doing that no less than a thousand times and could almost guess what the heated metal would feel like on his tongue. Or against the back of his teeth as he tugged lightly on the embedded adornment.

Links tucked himself into his pants and unclipped a length of chain from one of a dozen pockets.

Eli tensed, preparing to tear all three of the fuckers limb from limb if they so much as hurt one of the nonexistent hairs on Alanso's head. Instead of anything sinister, Links let the length fall, heavy, onto Alanso's biceps then drew it upward until it draped over his wrist. The implication of restraint was all that was required.

"Stay still, *cariño*. Let my boys treat you nice."

As if the chain weighed a ton, Alanso obeyed, not moving a fraction of an inch. To see the fiery man yield made Eli's dick drip. Slickness eased the shuttling of his fist over his length. Too much of that and he'd shoot all over the weeds at his feet before they'd even gotten to the juicy shit.

"Come on," he whispered.

Alanso's hips lifted, begging for something he likely didn't understand. Links had no trouble diagnosing a case of unrequited desire. "Phil, put your hand on his cock. Squeeze him nice and tight. You can stroke him a little. Don't you dare get him off yet."

"Yes, sir." The dude seemed to enjoy taking orders as much as he would relish being the recipient of the prescribed treatment. Eli's cock leaked, the droplet splashing into the soil.

"And Ronnie, push those legs wide as they'll go, considering our slut still has his pants around his ankles and those hot fucking motorcycle boots on. I bet you really ride, don't you?"

Alanso nodded. His eyes scrunched closed as his new cohorts assaulted him with pleasure. Knees splayed, soles of his feet touching, he gave them plenty of room to operate.

"That's it." Links tweaked Alanso's other nipple before returning his hand to Al's head and stroking him lightly enough to belie his gruff commands. "Now, Ronnie, get your face in those balls. Don't be prissy either. Fucking slather them with your tongue. Soak him. Let your spit run down his crack. Get his hole nice and drenched."

Eli thought someone had knocked the wind from him. What if they tried to fuck Alanso? Was he ready for that? Would they hurt him?

Could Eli stand by and watch them penetrate his best friend?

Something in him roared. That right should have been his.

Except he'd wasted the opportunity.

If he could do it all over…

Alanso writhed when Ronnie slurped his sac into his mouth and pulled lightly. Phil's fingers rhythmically squeezed and released Alanso's cock, teasing the bottom of his fat head.

From his outpost, Eli could detect the flaring of Alanso's nostrils. A tiny smear of blood emerged on his lip when he gnawed a section between his teeth. Probably trying his damnedest not to shoot.

Phil took it upon himself to nuzzle Alanso's belly. The chiseled abs couldn't have provided much pillow for the slender man's cheek. He watched up close and personal as his buddy followed instructions. Ronnie buried his nose beneath Alanso's heavy *cojones*. He went to town on the sensitive spot between the delicate orbs and Al's ass.

In the moonlight, Eli watched saliva drip toward the shadows between Alanso's thighs. He imagined the impromptu lube coating his rear entrance.

"Just do it already," Alanso barked.

The desperation in his directive startled Eli. Who could resist that invitation? Apparently, he had. What a fucking idiot. Why had he done that again?

He swore he couldn't remember a valid fucking reason.

Not one.

But he'd had so many.

Hadn't he?

Shit, this was bad.

"You're not ready to be fucked." Links squashed the flicker of hope in Ronnie's eyes.

He almost seemed to glance in the direction of Eli's hiding spot. King Cobra froze, his hand grinding to a halt on his cock.

Until the older man returned his laser intensity to the guys he orchestrated once more.

"Don't tell me what I can take." Alanso practically spit at them. "I've had enough of other peoples' judgments on my sex life. If I say I want to be fucked, that's what I want. What does a guy have to do to get a dick in his ass? *Me cago en diez!* Doesn't anyone want me?"

Eli tipped forward. The hand not cradling his erection landed on his knee for support.

The plea sliced through his guts like a rusty knife.

He deserved a thousand more cuts if he'd inflicted that clear pain on Alanso without even realizing it. Of course that's what Alanso would assume. That he was unwanted. Again. Shit. Fuck. Damn.

"You come back in two weeks, you'll have all the cock you can handle. Including mine." Links shook Alanso's shoulder. "*After* you've worn a plug a few days and maybe tried a smaller toy. No way am I letting your first time rip you up so you decide you don't like it. Sorry, *cariño.* You're going to have to settle for Ronnie's finger tonight."

"Argh. Fine. Fuck. Something. Whatever. Now. Please." Alanso had abandoned all semblance of grace. Raw desire ripped through the glade. The threat of a forest fire was high as he scorched everything, and everyone, around him with his passion.

"A little treat to warm you up." A smile tipped up one corner of Links' mouth. "Ronnie is great with his tongue."

"Down there?" Alanso's eyes widened.

Eli would have chuckled if he weren't so afraid of ruining the moment or causing an accidental misfire. Riding the edge of arousal, he couldn't take much more stimulation. The sights and sounds were nearly enough alone.

"You have no idea..." Phil petted Alanso, keeping him mostly in place when Ronnie's tongue licked a path from his balls to his ass.

"*Dios Mío! Dios! Dios!*" To hell with stealth. The park rang with Alanso's prayers. For more, Eli was sure.

Moist slurps accompanied the stream of mangled Spanish spilling from the guy who surrendered to his fantasies. So fast and furious, Eli couldn't keep up. He got the gist of the litany as Ronnie wiggled his face between those tight cheeks.

"I can feel him getting harder, Links." Phil paused his manipulation of Alanso's cock. The skin there had passed blush and moved on to an almost-painful-looking purple. "Don't disappoint him. He's not going to make it much longer."

"Go ahead." The man nodded to Ronnie. "Work your pinky in him."

"No. Bigger." Alanso gasped.

"Fine. You stubborn little *maricón*." Links shook his head with an affectionate grin on his face. "Give him your middle finger, Ronnie."

Alanso grunted when the man between his legs wasted no time in complying. A hiss escaped his clenched jaw and the white teeth he bared.

"Take it." Links didn't cut him any slack. "You're going to get what you wanted. And then some, I think."

There it was again, a peek in Eli's direction. *Shit!*

Stopping then would have been impossible. He choked up on his cock and refused to break his stare. Not from Links and certainly not from the gorgeous sight of Alanso's awakening.

"Damn, he's tight." Ronnie grunted. "Been a long time since I had an ass like that."

"Hey." Phil shot him a glare.

"No worries, I like your ass plenty." He beamed up at his partner. "In fact, I'm about to show you how much. Give me two minutes."

"More like thirty seconds," Links amended.

"If that." Phil returned his attention to Alanso. He waited until Ronnie signaled him with a nod.

"I'm in as far as I can go." He glanced up at the other two guys. "Gotta really work."

"Good." The encouragement spurred all three men to please Links more. "Ronnie, fuck him. Nice and slow. In and out all the way. Phil, lean in closer. You know you like a nice facial. I bet this is going to be the best you've had. Start tugging on him. Just a little."

Alanso made noises Eli had never heard from him. Not even the time an entire case of motor oil had toppled from a cabinet and smooshed his hand between it and the frame of a vintage Corvette, breaking several bones in the process.

"That's right, *cariño*." Surprisingly tender, Links encouraged Alanso to surrender. "You're safe here. Let it all out. We understand. No one's going to make you hide again, are they?"

"No!" Alanso roared into the night.

Phil's hand rippled along the shaft in his grip and Ronnie went double time.

They all held their breath for a split second. Then Alanso exploded. He screamed, "Eli! Sally!"

And those two little words ripped Eli apart from the inside out.

He shuddered and his cock lurched. His balls felt as though they might flip inside out, they drew so tight to his frame.

The iron tang of blood flavored his mouth. He kept silent despite the tsunami of pleasure, longing and fear laying waste to everything in its path, leaving his insides hollow. His future uncertain. Jet after jet of come poured from him, shooting hard enough from his dick to get lost in the brush.

They came together, even if Alanso didn't know it.

All along, Alanso shuddered. His body jerked as though he'd been electrocuted. He shouted, cursed, prayed, gave thanks and supplied inarticulate expressions of his ultimate relief.

The sight brought Eli to his knees.

His head hung. Moisture scorched his eyes.

He'd reduced his best friend to yielding to a stranger's touch. This couldn't possibly be right. And now he'd probably fucked things up beyond repair. Struggling to get his breathing under control, he listened to the men emerging from their trance, less than ten feet away.

"I wondered for so long. But shit, I never imagined it could be *that* good." Alanso threw one arm over his face. His chest billowed as if he'd unloaded the entire week's supply shipment by himself, in record time.

If Eli didn't know better he might have thought he saw the sheen of tears in Al's eyes before he obscured them.

"Welcome to our world." Phil rubbed Alanso's shoulder. "You did great for your first time. If you find yourself in the neighborhood again…"

Eli regained his feet and took a few steps forward, unable to stay away. *No*. Next time it would be his finger in Alanso's ass. Or better yet, his cock.

"Thank you," Alanso murmured. He deflated as if every bone in his body melted in the wake of his release. How tightly had he been strung that Eli hadn't even realized…

"So, who's Eli?" Phil asked quietly. "And Sally?"

"Huh?" Alanso peeked from below his arm, blinking out of his daze.

"You called for them when you busted." He smiled softly. "Whoever they are, I hope they figure out how lucky they are before it's too late."

"I know." Eli cleared his throat.

Alanso shot up like a rocket. He scrambled to draw his clothes into place.

Links, Phil and Ronnie formed a wall between him and Eli. The man could win over even the toughest crowds in a matter of minutes. Jesus, he was amazing. And he didn't get it. Never had fully.

"It's okay, guys. He's a friend." Alanso cleared his throat. "My best friend."

Eli hated how Alanso cowered when he approached. He didn't hesitate to offer a hand. He hated looming over the guy.

When Al's chocolate gaze flicked upward from Eli's boots, it paused. His pupils dilated even further than the night had mandated.

Eli glanced down and spotted a thick, pearly strand of come he must have launched onto the thigh of his jeans. *Shit.*

Alanso reached up. He hesitated, as if Eli might run again, before touching the tip of one finger to the wet line. He swiped a trace of the fluid from the leg of Eli's pants and brought it to his mouth. A purr escaped from his throat as he tasted Eli's desire.

"Can we talk about this at home?" Alanso gained his feet and stared directly into Eli's eyes. He didn't blink once as Eli tried to put everything he felt into words yet failed miserably.

All he could do was nod his head.

When a couple of creases appeared at the corners of Alanso's eyes, Eli reacted on instinct. He thrust his hands out and cupped the shorter man's cheeks. He drew the guy to him and crashed their mouths together.

Their teeth clicked once before they found their rhythm, both used to leading. Alanso whimpered into Eli's mouth. He couldn't help but try to soothe the frantic questions he'd unintentionally inspired.

Eli forced himself to slow down. For Alanso's sake. He used every sliver of self-control he had to harness the energy sparking between them as if they stood at the center of an enormous Tesla coil.

Tempering urgency with richness, he glided his mouth over Alanso's.

The vague mint taste didn't stop Eli from detecting the distinct zest of his best friend. Or the delicious flavor of the promise they sealed with their very first kiss.

How different it was to make out with a guy. This man.

And yet the same.

But way better than anything he'd felt before.

They made a few more passes of lips over lips. Until Eli's lungs burned and the edges of his vision turned blacker than the night could account for.

Reluctantly, they split. Alanso's mouth made one last bid for attention, nipping Eli's lower lip as he retreated.

They stared at each other.

"I'm sorry," Eli breathed against Alanso's mouth, hating the remnants of latex he tasted on his friend's lips. "I'll make this right. I swear."

"*Hijo de puta*, you'd better," Alanso snarled before stepping away, a glint of mistrust in his eyes.

"I guess this means we won't be seeing you again." Phil kicked a rock idly.

"I hope not." Alanso grinned and fist bumped Links before jogging up the hill toward his bike. He called over his shoulder, "Thanks."

Eli groaned. It was going to be a long ride home, watching that tight ass fly down the road in front of him.

CHAPTER FIVE

Alanso swung his leg over his bike and clomped up the metal stairs at the rear of Hot Rods without waiting for Eli to park his Cobra in the personal bays the rest of the group reserved for their rides. His bed called loud and clear. Given the chaos of his thoughts and the ragged emotion chasing on the heels of his experiment, he thought it'd be best if he avoided a confrontation tonight.

God only knew what he'd say when all of his insides were laid bare. He felt like he was turned inside out and everyone could see his guts, what made him tick and the dumb hope causing his heart to pound.

He had to think.

Or maybe getting in his head too much was the fucking problem. Deliberating hadn't done him any good over the past several months.

Seriously, there was no mistaking the tongue Eli had shoved in his mouth before spinning on his heels and commanding Alanso home.

But he hadn't been exactly affectionate either, had he?

Begrudging intimacy wasn't going to cut it anymore. He refused to settle. Or walk around feeling like he'd done something wrong.

Links had it right. Alanso didn't plan to hide ever again.

Except maybe just this one night. Until he figured out what to say to the five guys and one smoking hot woman staring at him as he opened the door to their common room a teensy bit too fast. The knob slipped from his grasp, allowing the door to hit the wall as he flew inside. A black-and-white picture of their first restoration job fell off the wall. The glass cracked as it hit the hardwood floor they'd installed a few years ago.

Just like that, something inside him shattered along with it.

His eyes flickered first to Sally. Worry lines around her pretty green eyes only amped him up more. This tension between him and Eli had affected the entire group in some way. From where he lounged on the couch beside her, Carver put his hand on her shoulder.

The movie they'd been watching droned in the background.

Roman, Holden, Kaige and Bryce set their cards on the table despite the large pot resting between them. Big, usually quiet, Bryce broke the silence. "You okay, Alanso?"

"No."

Roman's eyes widened and Holden scooted his chair around so he could catch the show too. In an instant, Sally rose and started to cross the sweeping area. The second floor of the garage was enormous. A complete blank slate had allowed them to slice the space into the rooms they needed to house them all while leaving a big-ass kitchen and this common ground.

Fortunately, the size of the living room gave Alanso opportunity to evade Mustang Sally's outstretched arms. He put a beat-up leather recliner between them.

"Don't." He shook his head. She couldn't touch him after where he'd been. What he'd done.

Tears shimmered in her eyes, obscuring jade behind pools of crystal. "What happened? What's wrong? Where's Eli?"

Relief washed through the gang when the door opened for the second time in as many minutes and their King Cobra came home.

"Who broke the picture?" He stepped toward the shards on the floor. Would he sweep them up? Alanso didn't think he could.

None of them could put it back together now. It was too late. The damage had been done.

"I did." Alanso didn't recognize the tone of his own voice. "Leave it. I'll get it before I head out in the morning."

"What?" Sally rounded the chair. "Where are you going?"

Alanso kept pace, never letting her close the distance. "It doesn't matter. But I'm tired of pretending to be something I'm not just to fit in."

Sally propped her hands on her hips. She looked damn cute when she got pissed. Not that it happened often. "The hell're you talking about? Did *he* tell you to get out?"

She jabbed a finger in Eli's direction.

"You know better than that, Sally." Eli's response came quiet yet sure.

"Shut up." Her snap at the garage owner raised a few brows in the room. "You've fucked up enough already, haven't you? Somebody damn well better tell us what's going on. Keeping us in the dark is a shitty thing to do. Since when do we hide stuff from each other? Afraid we're going to kick your ass, Eli? I'm starting to think you really deserve it."

Alanso appreciated her loyalty. No questions asked. She'd always have his back.

Which is why he felt extra lame when he rounded on her as she crept closer again.

But having her near confused him all over again, just when he'd thought he'd found some answers.

"Stop! Don't you get it? I don't like *chocha*." He drew a ragged breath, knowing he had to say the word. For himself. "Sally, I'm gay!"

Holden laughed first.

He flat out snorted as he rocked in his chair. Several beer bottles scattered on the table in front of him when his arm knocked into them. The clatter echoed off the high ceilings with exposed metal beams.

Sally froze. She tipped her head as she scrutinized him. Her gaze roamed over him inch by inch, as if one of his tattoos had secretly proclaimed his orientation all this time and she'd missed it.

Roman shot up from his chair. He paced behind the poker table. As usual, he didn't say anything right away, but Alanso could practically hear the wheels turning in his mind. What conclusion were they working toward? Would he accept a gay guy in their mix?

Carver piped up from the couch. Not in disgust. With pure curiosity, which was harder to drum up protective anger toward.

"I'm confused, Al. It was less than six months ago that I walked in on you, in our laundry room, fucking that check-out girl from the grocery store. There wasn't any faking the way you pile-drived her."

"Hell, this place isn't soundproof. We've *all* heard you making women scream. And that damned Spanish. Wraps them around your dick every time. What's this really about?" Kaige grinned, his golden dreadlocks dancing around his head as he shrugged. "Dude. You almost had me for a second there."

"I'm not joking, *cabrón*." He scrubbed his hand over his head. "Okay, maybe not *maricón*. What do you call it? Bi. Something. Whatever. I sucked a guy's dick tonight and I liked it. Label that whatever the fuck you want."

"You should have waited outside for me," Eli murmured. "This isn't the time or place for this discussion. Let's take a walk. Cool off."

"Fuck you." Alanso wrenched away from Cobra. "I've had enough of secrets. They deserve to know why I'm not welcome. Why everything went to hell."

"You're always welc—"

"No, I'm not." Refusing to settle for half-alive wasn't an option anymore.

While he was distracted, Mustang Sally snuck in. He flinched when she wrapped her arms around his waist and laid her cheek between his shoulder blades. "We love you, Alanso. It doesn't matter who you choose to have sex with. Why would you think we're so judgmental?"

Whether it was the heat of her embrace or the enormous open heart she flashed them all, arousal—the same familiar longing that had plagued him lately in the presence of his de facto family—flared around him. The inappropriate thoughts heated his cheeks and had him staring at the floor.

Not one of the guys uttered a peep.

"Because Eli is." He hated the trembling in his worn-out muscles. It transmitted his exhaustion and fear to Sally as clearly as if he'd painted the torment in the bright colors she loved so much. "He's been keeping me gagged for months."

And didn't that image rouse his cock? Damn thing wouldn't behave. Seriously? After the best fucking night of his life? Well, second best if you counted the session with the crew.

"What?" Roman stood farthest away, but there was no way he had misheard.

"You're ashamed of him?" Bryce took a step closer, cracking his knuckles. "Cobra, what the fuck?"

"Hell, no." Eli rounded on the beefy guy. "You don't understand the situation."

"Of course not, *coño*. Because you haven't shared any of it with them. How could they know what we saw? What we did?" Weeks and weeks of rage exploded from Alanso at once. "You refused to be honest about it. You're a fucking coward. I didn't imagine your cock in my hand or your tongue in my mouth, did I?"

"Holy shit." Kaige plopped into his seat. "Is this the Twilight Zone or something?"

"No. You did not." Eli stepped closer.

Alanso couldn't have retreated even if he'd wanted to with Sally plastered to his back, sobbing quietly. He knew how much conflict upset her. Still, he couldn't stop the snowball they'd set rolling down this mountain of angst.

"Well, at least I'm not crazy *and* gay," he spat.

"Look, if you keep saying that like it's a bad word, you're going to be fighting with more than Cobra." Holden surprised them all by getting fired up. The usually affable guy rarely took a stand on serious issues. "You're not the only one in this room who's hooked up with a dude. I just never had some kind of emo crisis about it. Do what feels good and fuck anyone who tells you not to. What the hell's so hard about that?"

Alanso's stare whipped to his friend. Could it be true? All this time he'd spent not confiding in them he could have had an ally. It was partially his fault. Not everything could be blamed on Cobra. That asshole.

"Nothing." He cleared his throat. "It's how I plan to live from now on. Like from right this second. And it's how the crew does it too."

"The crew?" Sally tensed around him. "Joe and his guys? What do they have to do with this?"

"Alanso..." Cobra hissed out a warning.

"Quit that." Bryce winged a clay poker chip at Eli. It bounced off his corded biceps. "Let him talk."

Alanso swallowed hard. "When Dave was in the accident and we went down to help, the crew was a mess. Kate and Morgan were pregnant and having a rough time. They were all torn up. Terrified he wasn't going to make it. We finished with the insurance paperwork earlier than expected so we met Joe, Morgan, Kate and Mike back at their house where the women were resting. Or so we thought."

Eli hadn't blinked once. It was as if he could visualize the scene they'd walked in on as clearly as Alanso could. The day replayed like a movie on endless loop in his mind.

"Cobra didn't want to wake them. Morgan had practically passed out at the hospital and the guys weren't hanging in there much better. So he picked the lock. We snuck in." Alanso couldn't stop himself from licking his lips. "Joe was fucking Morgan on a mattress. Right there on the floor of the living room."

"Guess she was feeling better." Kaige's eyebrows wiggled.

"They were helping her get there." Alanso nodded. "Taking away some of the fear and comforting her."

"Who's *they*?" Roman spoke up.

"Kate watched while Mike and Joe got it on with her." Alanso couldn't help the boner that started to rise. He hoped they wouldn't notice.

"Damn." Bryce rubbed his chest. "That's fucking hot. Kate was cool with it?"

"Hell yeah." He thought back to the serene smile on her face. "She wasn't up for sex with Mike just then. But she didn't want him to suffer. I could see how much she loved him. All of them. While she cheered them on."

Eli still hadn't budged. Light brown hair stuck out in a messy array, courtesy of his convertible. He breathed hard at the memories. He stood rigid as Alanso spilled his family's secrets.

Alanso had talked to the crew enough lately to know they didn't mind him sharing the details of their alternative lifestyle. Hell, they'd threatened to call the garage and enlighten the rest of the Hot Rods if he didn't do it soon.

"I always knew Morgan was a lucky bitch," Sally whispered, squeezing him tighter. If she didn't let up he might suffocate. He wouldn't mind. Her hug soothed his heart.

"I assumed because of your moms..." Alanso paused.

"After how I grew up, it seems kind of normal to have more than one partner." Sally hardly ever talked about her childhood in rural Utah. "That wasn't why I ran away. I didn't like being brainwashed. Or forced."

He dropped his shoulder, allowing her to swing around to his side and tuck under his arm. Holding her in return helped him finish. Especially when Kaige asked, "What does any of this have to do with you being gay?"

"Cause what we busted in on was only the beginning." Eli's raspy answer startled them all, if the dead silence was any indication. "Go ahead. You've gone this far. Finish it."

Alanso certainly didn't argue. "After they'd satisfied Morgan, you could tell Mike hadn't had enough. You know how everything falls to him."

Though he spoke of the head of the crew, Alanso stared into Eli's eyes as he elaborated.

"He takes on tons of responsibility. Protects them. Worries. Loves them all." A deep breath stretched his ribs.

Sally rubbed his back with one hand.

"Mike asked Joe if he could fuck him. Joe let him. It was like he gave up everything to Mike, allowed him to take all the anxiety and relaxed for the first time since I'd seen him. And for a while Mike had the situation under control again. The whole time, Morgan made out with Joe and helped him get off. They were in it together. Kate..."

Alanso peeked up at Eli, who didn't try to shush him again.

"She played with me and Cobra. We did stuff. To each other."

A strangled groan left Sally's milky white throat. Whether it was approving or disgusted, he couldn't tell.

"And I liked it." Alanso gulped. "A lot."

Afraid to glance up, a weight lifted from his shoulders when Eli said, "I did too."

Kaige coughed around the slug of beer he'd taken to wet his throat. "Holy shit, guys. Well, I have to say of all the things we put in the pool as reasons for your bad mood...no one had *that*."

"I sort of did." Sally peeked at him from her spot against his chest. She laid her palm over his pounding heart. "I had lack of pussy. I know how you boys get when you hit a dry spell. And neither of you have been going out lately."

"You keeping track of us now?" Alanso couldn't say why it bothered him that she paid such close attention. Maybe it shamed him because he didn't care for any of the women he'd shared sheets with as much as he did for her.

Standing there, with her and Eli so close, sandwiching him between them, had him breaking out in a sweat.

"Excuse me, guys." Carver raised his hand, being ridiculous as always.

"What?" Eli growled.

"If *you* liked it...and *he* liked it...what the motherfuck is the problem here?" He scratched the stubble on his jaw.

"Good question." Alanso's spine straightened. "Apparently, Cobra only approves when he's hot. Afterward, he's horrified."

"Don't put words in my mouth." The corner of Eli's eye twitched, as it did when he got thermonuclear angry. It didn't happen very often, but when it did...

"I don't need fancy talk to explain when you avoid me like I gave you herpes or some shit. You fucking insisted I not tell them what happened and acted like I'd killed someone.

Even tonight, you must have watched. You were on the scene a fucking second after I finished. But you didn't bother to join in or try to break their fingers for touching me. It's pretty obvious you don't give a shit."

Sally interjected, "I don't believe that, Alanso. I'm sorry he's made you feel unwanted. He's a dumbass, yes. But he loves you. We all do."

"You're our brother," Roman affirmed.

"And *that's* my problem." Eli latched on to the excuse. "How can I want him? Or more? Any of you? All of you. Because believe me, I do. I wish you all could have seen what we did. I think you might like it too. I remember those nights...when we were younger, undisciplined, dumber... There were some close calls."

He met each person's gaze for a moment or two before moving on to the next.

"What you saw affected you as much as it did Al." Bryce nodded, moving closer. "I can see where it would disturb you to blur the lines. You've always thought you had to look out for us."

"You realize we're plenty capable of holding our own, right?" Kaige chuckled. Hell, he'd single-handedly started and finished bar brawls regularly back when they were in their wilder days. "We're close, yes. Something more than family. And if this is what you two want, I'd be willing to dip a toe in and see where it goes. If it doesn't work for someone, or several people, we don't have to pursue it."

"I'd like to watch," Sally whispered. A few of the guys mumbled their agreement. When she lifted her face toward Alanso, he thought maybe for a second she would keep stretching onto her tiptoes and put that dark red mouth lined with something even darker too close to his. Tonight had left him with no self-control intact. He stepped out of her hold. Unfortunately, that left him within Eli's reach.

Instead of making a grab for him, Cobra closed his eyes. He stood there, breathing hard for a moment or two before his lids fluttered open and he focused his brilliant blue laser stare on Alanso. "Get over here and kiss me."

Injustice triggered his stubborn streak. It didn't seem fair that he'd had to beg for months only to give in immediately to Eli's whims. "I'm not your bitch."

"Don't you wish you were?" Cobra canted his head. His high cheekbones were accentuated by the devilish smile Alanso knew so well. *Dios*, he'd missed that look. Homesickness roiled in his guts. He'd prayed for this man. And he didn't care if it made him a pussy, he caved.

"Sometimes." Alanso squared himself to his best friend, coming face-to-face. "But mostly I wonder what it would be like to make you forget about the world for one fucking moment. What if I could take away your obsession with the bills, worry about your dad's loneliness, the look you get on your face any time one of us doesn't feel well or, God forbid, has to go to the doctor? What would it be like to see you carefree? *That's* what I wish."

"Never gonna happen, Al." Roman sighed.

"Prove him wrong." The dare hung in the air. Eli knew damn well Alanso couldn't resist a challenge like that. "Go ahead."

Alanso didn't recall deciding to give in. One instant he was floundering, his whole life about to change—for better or worse he couldn't tell yet. The next, he'd stepped forward, grabbed Eli's head between his palms and tugged until the taller guy yielded.

Before their mouths could crush onto each other again, Eli murmured, "I'm sorry."

This time, when they met, something was different.

Sure, the urgency remained. A rough massage at the back of Eli's skull nudged him closer. Alanso practically climbed the garage owner despite their friends witnessing his undeniable craving for the guy he groped.

Yet their lips told another story. Eli didn't advance. He allowed Alanso to take charge of their exchange. Instead of powerful nips or the lashing of tongues, they traded swipes of soft, wet flesh against the same.

Eli fed a groan into Alanso's open mouth. He went still and calm. His movements turned fluid. The change spurred Alanso to escalate their encounter. The hard wall of Cobra's chest met his as they fused together full-length. And only when his hands roamed from that short, tousled hair past strong shoulders to a narrow waist and finally to Eli's gorgeous ass did he realize the shafts trapped between them were equally hard.

Hell, it felt as if Cobra really did have a massive trouser snake if the bulge poking Alanso's flexed abs was any indication. In the background, someone whistled.

Coming to his senses, Alanso opened his eyes. He imprinted the peace and desire in Eli's expression on his memory before he ripped away.

Cobra stumbled.

Carver appeared from beside them to brace the garage owner. It seemed he'd elected for a ringside seat to their little show. Sally clasped Eli's other arm, steadying him on his feet where he swayed.

"Great idea. It's time for bed." Their leader was back, and he had a mission.

"You think just because you rock at tonsil hockey, you're going to sleep with me tonight?" Alanso shoved away from Eli's chest. "Fuck off. I'm still pissed. It's going to take a hell of a lot more than one fucking tongue tango to convince me that you deserve a shot with me."

Eli grinned, wide and slow. "You think I'm a good kisser?"

"Kiss my ass, Cobra. *No me jodes.*" He stalked toward his room, which shared a wall with Eli's, trying not to remember how Ronnie had done just that earlier, while Cobra observed from the shadows.

"Wow, Al. Maybe you really are a chick under all those tattoos." Holden got smacked upside the head by Roman for his smartassery. Sally tossed in a defense for her kind too. She wasn't a head-game player like most women they'd run across.

A double salute from Alanso's middle fingers, without checking the rearview for reaction, marked his exit. The day had drained him. In more ways than one.

Maybe tomorrow he could process it all.

Until then, sleep sounded heavenly.

He locked his hallway door, stripped to bare-assed-naked and took a minute to brush his teeth in the bathroom he shared with Cobra. It didn't occur to him that his mind had stopped racing for the first time in months, making it easy to crash into his pillows and drift off.

CHAPTER SIX

"**H**ey, that was the most interesting weeknight we've had in a few years." Holden clapped a hand on Carver's shoulder as the guys and Sally huddled around Eli. "We're getting old. Rusty."

Eli didn't even bother to level one of his shut-the-hell-up glares in Holden's direction. Suddenly, he felt weary. Unable to fight the tide that'd been dragging him out to sea.

"You gonna say something?" Kaige took up a spot near Bryce as they closed rank. "Eli, man, you all right?"

"I just want to make it clear that if any of you has an issue with what went down tonight, you bring it to me. Don't you dare shit on Alanso because of this." He bristled.

"I think the only guy here who's got a problem with it is you." Roman's stern tone didn't surprise anyone. As the oldest of their group, he had lived the hard life longer than most of them had, since Eli's family had given them sanctuary one by one as they'd wandered into the youth shelter Eli's mom had worked to build.

Roman had been a different matter. To this day, he worshipped Eli's father—Tom—for not calling the cops on him when he'd caught the young man trying to hotwire his truck. Instead, he'd offered a loan he never expected to be repaid and a job pumping gas at the garage and service station so Roman wouldn't have to stoop to petty theft ever again.

He'd busted his ass to fulfill his debt in record time, and he'd been there ever since.

The deep grooves around his mouth, his calculating eyes and the smell of hard liquor on his breath all combined to make him someone you didn't want to mess with in a dark alley.

"What are you planning to do now?" Sally patted Eli's chest, snapping his attention to the situation at hand. The fire in her eyes guaranteed he'd better answer this one right or risk her knee meeting his balls. She was quick and fierce. It'd hurt like hell.

"I—I have no idea."

Stunned silence echoed around the cavernous room, designed to hold them all comfortably.

"You've always got the roadmap." Carver's jaw hung open wider at Eli's indecision than it had at Alanso's dramatic declaration.

"Not for this." Eli scrubbed his knuckles over his eyes. "I don't have a fucking clue what to do. I know what I want, but I don't know what's right. Not for Al or for any of us. I realize this is all new to you guys, so I think you should take some time to really think about the implications."

Most of the Hot Rods nodded. Sally shook her head. "All I want to know is—do you plan to keep things between the two of you or expand like the crew did?"

"I can't say, Sally." He shrugged. Partly it depended on what the rest of the gang thought. He owed them time to process what they'd just witnessed. The lack of direction made him feel like his internal compass had crapped out. He'd always known where he was headed and marched toward his goals without pause. Now...he spun in circles. Changing his mind every five seconds.

Go to Alanso. That voice screamed loudest, but he resisted.

Back off.

Test the waters with the Hot Rods.

Leave them alone.

Show them how much you love them.

Don't fuck up what you have.

Indecision was driving him insane. Oscillating between two polar opposites, he felt like a piston moving back and forth at an ungodly RPM. He hadn't been this stuck since the time they'd attempted to drive one of their finds down the muddy, unpaved driveway leading from the estate sale they'd snagged the bargain at. It'd taken all of them pushing together to break free of that mire.

"Cobra, go talk to your dad," Bryce suggested.

"About this?" He backed up a step, then another. "No way. What am I going to tell him? That I think I'm into guys now? That I'm having some early midlife crisis? Jesus."

"You'll know what to say when you get there." Sally closed the gap between them and put her hand on his forearm. He studied her nails. She'd redone them again tonight. Now they were a hot pink color in two finishes—matte on the bed and glossy on the tip. Subtle yet not. Always interesting. Just like the paint jobs she designed and applied to the cars they restored. "He'll help you think it through."

Rather than argue those points, Eli picked something simpler. "It's after midnight. He's in bed by now, I'm sure."

"Nah," Kaige disagreed. "He stopped by for a few beers before. We told him something was up with you and Al. Actually, he kind of insisted that you come see him when you got home. Sorry, dude."

Holden jabbed his fingers into the mini-blinds and separated two of the slats to peer into the night. "The porch light is on. He's staying up for you. Better not keep him waiting any longer. Don't waste the chance to lean on what you've got. None of the rest of us are that lucky unless we borrow your dad."

"Crap!" For the first time since his curfew days, Eli suffered a moment of panic over walking through that door at this ungodly hour. "Fine. Fuck. I'm going. Who's opening with me tomorrow? Shit...today. Kaige? Carver? Get your asses to bed. Nobody should be dragging when we're working with the lifts and equipment. We'll talk about this more this weekend."

"Promise?" Sally looked up at him with wide eyes.

"Damn it, yes." With that he spun on his heel and jogged down the stairs, across the lawn and onto the porch of his father's home. He usually loved having the guy so close. But tonight, he wasn't sure their proximity played to his advantage.

Was he ready to share everything? Even if he didn't know what all that entailed yet?

He trusted his father above anyone else in the world. The death of Eli's mom had brought them closer. Almost more like friends than father and son. They'd been there for each other, then for the Hot Rods they'd discovered and inherited in the years following.

"In here, Eli," his dad called from the living room as if the flash of the TV, which probably aired some travel documentary, didn't highlight the way.

"Hi." Nothing else came to mind.

"So, you want to tell me what had you two kids peeling out of here like harebrains? Those damn engines are loud enough to have all our neighbors calling and complaining to me." Tom London didn't beat around the bush.

"Since when do you give a shit what Mrs. Shoff thinks of us anyway?"

"You're right, I don't give a damn." Tom clicked off the TV and angled toward Eli. "But *I've* had enough of this sulking. I want to know what's wrong."

Eli sank into a comfortably worn recliner, rested his elbows on his knees and put his head in his hands. "It's complicated, Dad."

"I'm not stupid. I'll follow." Tom crossed his arms.

"Are you pissed?" He narrowed his eyes at the rare irritation his father seemed to be barely containing. This wasn't good. Hell, was he screwing up with everyone he loved lately?

"Kind of. Disappointed, actually."

Eli hadn't heard that tone since a bunch of them had gotten busted racing for money on a dangerous road one night in his early twenties. He'd hoped never to earn that slimy feeling in his gut again. "Why?"

"I thought you trusted me." The statement rang with accusation.

"I do." Eli wasn't lying. His dad had always been there for him. Maybe he'd been stupid not to come here sooner for this talk. "It's just...my issue affects more than me. Not sure it's right to drag everyone else's skeletons out in the open."

"Is one of the Hot Rods in trouble?" Tom leaned forward in his seat. "You've got to tell me if they are. I can help."

"No. Nothing like that." He hated the relief that washed over his dad's face. His dad had really been worried. And without facts to go on, he'd probably assumed the worst. "It's kind of, maybe, good news. Things are changing. There's a relationship thing happening. But it could cause some issues in the gang. That's what's bothering me. I don't want to alienate anybody. I can't lose any of them over this."

"Are you trying to say a couple of you are pairing off?" A smile tipped the edges of Tom's mouth for an instant. Then his dad rubbed his temples as if he had a headache. "I've wondered for a while which of you was going to break up the band."

"What's that supposed to mean?"

"You know, which guy was going to fall for Sally first." He shrugged. "It was bound to happen sooner or later. She's gorgeous, funny, tough, mysterious, a little sad. A potent combination. You kids screw around plenty, but not one of you has ever found something meaningful in a partner. Why do you think that is, son?"

"Very few people get as lucky as you and Mom." The reminder of what they'd lost hurt them both. But it was the truth. The way his parents had looked at each other... Hell, his mom's heart monitor had soared every time his dad had showed up to take a shift by her bed at the hospital.

"Maybe." Even now Tom smiled when he thought of his wife. He still wore his wedding ring. Swore he'd go to his grave with the simple band hugging his finger. "Personally, I think you've been looking in all the wrong places. Or maybe refusing to admit what you already know. After all, Joe and the crew seem to have done pretty fine for themselves, haven't they?"

"Yeah." Eli cleared his throat. "About them..."

His dad didn't come to his rescue. He waited the pause out.

"Shit. Dad, did you know they're into group stuff?" He winced as he considered the reaction he'd get or what the guys might do when they realized he'd spilled the beans on their complex relationship.

"It wasn't obvious?" Tom reclined in his chair, spreading his legs wider as he relaxed. "Hell, for a second there you had me worried. I thought you were going to tell me something awful."

"Wait, how could you tell?" *And doesn't it freak you out?* he wanted to add.

"It's obvious from the complete comfort they've always had around each other. Plus the way their wives folded right into that bond. Even if that weren't enough, it would have been impossible to ignore right about the time James and Neil blabbed everything to me. They were worried when all the other guys had found a woman that the crew wouldn't get together anymore." Tom waved a hand in the air. "Like the guys would be able to stay away after so many years together. I remember the days of being twisted up so tight you can't think straight, but seeing it from the outside... Yeah, a whole lot of drama over nothing. When it's right, it's right, and that's all that matters in the end."

"Oh. Well, fuck." Eli started to laugh. "I guess this might be easier than I thought to tell you, then. Maybe."

"Just spit it out already. Is it you or Alanso who's fooling around with Sally and making his best buddy jealous as hell?" Tom didn't usually gossip, but he scratched his head as he asked.

Eli closed his eyes, took a deep breath and borrowed a page out of Alanso's book. He'd fucking put it all right out there to the Hot Rods before. Eli admired him a little more after tonight. "Actually. It's Alanso and me who've kind of tangled it up a bit. Not as much as he wants, though. Not yet."

"Oh." Tom paused for a second. He blinked. "I see. I guess I don't quite understand why you boys are fighting then."

"That's all you're going to say about it?"

"I don't think I'm ready for details just yet." Tom chuckled. "Gotta give a guy a minute to work things out first. I'm not surprised you two love each other. Just not sure I figured you'd jump straight to that without easing your way in first. For so long I've wondered about Sally, I guess I didn't see it.

Actually...something happened when you went out there to help the crew. After the accident. Didn't it?"

Eli swallowed hard and nodded.

"This is starting to make sense." Tom tapped his fingers on his knee slowly. "I've been trying to figure out what changed. I thought maybe seeing their close call reminded you of your mom. That maybe you'd realized you don't get all the time in the world to waste, so you'd decided to make a move."

"Actually, I think that's kind of what happened to Alanso. Yes." Eli sighed.

"But you're being stubborn, aren't you?" Tom grunted. "It's all coming clear now. You dumbass. You pushed him away?"

"You *want* me to be gay?" Eli jumped to his feet, flinging his hands in the air. "Is everyone losing their fucking minds around here?"

"I love you no matter who you decide to be with, Eli." Tom also stood. He might have been an inch or two shorter than his son, but there was no mistaking his ranking in their family. "I don't think things are as simple as terms make them out to be. You've got something with those kids. It's been there since the beginning. Who am I to say what's right or wrong? It is how it is."

"But it's never been like *that* before." Eli paced the modest living room. "Why now?"

"Maybe you weren't ready." Tom caged in his son, dropping his hand on Eli's shoulder. "You've done a hell of a lot of growing up over the past ten years. Built your business, your friendships. You played around enough to know what you like. And you've helped them all get to a somewhat normal place. That took a long time. A lot of healing had to be done. I think somewhere, deep down, you know the gang is ready to take this next step."

"You get that I don't just want Alanso, right?" Eli clenched the fireplace mantle so hard his knuckles turned white. "I have no idea what exactly this is going to look like when it's all said and done, but I think it's bigger than him and me. Yeah, you're right. I have a major thing for Sally. I'm pretty damn sure Alanso does too."

"Dream big, son." Tom grinned. "But maybe you'd better start with Alanso if things between you are spiraling out of control. No more of this fighting. I hate to see that. It bothers all of you kids. Sets everyone on edge. They've had too much misery already in their lives to borrow more from you. Hell, you two are practically an old married couple anyway. Just without the sex. Might as well add the benefits."

"And I think that's where I draw the line when talking to my father." Eli was attempting to be mature about this, but he hadn't even slammed a shot or two before coming over here to dull the awkwardness. What had he been thinking?

"Yeah, me too." Tom nodded. "But I did win that round of chicken."

Eli laughed. He went with his gut and turned to hug his dad. "Thank you for understanding. I do know how lucky I am, by the way."

"So do I." Tom clutched him hard enough to crack a rib. After all he'd been through it would have been easy to turn sour, angry at the world. Yet he never had. He'd held tight to the good times he'd had and the legacy his wife had left. Because of him, the Hot Rods all had a home. "Now get the hell out of here so I can go to bed."

***

Eli flung his arm away from where it'd been curled over his face. It was no use. He couldn't sleep. Hadn't managed to stop thinking about what he'd seen at Chestnut Grove for more than three milliseconds since he climbed into bed. Especially since he knew Alanso was right there on the other side of the wall that was bookended by the headboards of their beds.

Plus, by some miracle, not only his friends but also his father approved of the dangerous liaison he'd plotted and replotted during the endless hours of darkness. With the first rays of morning that beamed through his window, Eli saw clearly what he'd like to do.

Hell, it'd be impossible to miss the tent made by his sheets over his rock-solid erection.

He could slip through the adjoining bathroom he and Alanso shared, into the dusk-shrouded midst of the other guy's lair. After pulling back the black silk sheets, he'd tuck himself in to steal some of his friend's warmth.

Sleepy, Alanso wouldn't stand a chance at resisting. He adored morning sex.

Of all the Hot Rods, he was one of the few likely to invite a woman to stay overnight. Probably because he liked opening his eyes and seeing his date hadn't left.

Eli slapped the mattress a few times, gearing himself up to action. Just when he had committed and kicked off his blankets, the rush of water hitting the tile of their shower stopped him short.

What the hell? Alanso didn't open today. Or ever, really. The rest of the guys knew he preferred a lazy start to the morning and left him to the late shift most times. Eli generally stayed the whole day, opening and closing, no matter how often they told him to get the fuck out of his own business to enjoy some time off.

Truth was, when you loved what you did, and who you did it with, it hardly felt like a job at all. This—making things right with the guy who mattered most to him—was hard work. And he was prepared to do whatever it took to fix the damage he'd inflicted.

He staggered into the bathroom, surprised by how stiff he was. Christ, he'd had massive hangovers less painful. Had he lain there completely tense all night?

The running shower made wet noises as Alanso got clean. The splashes guaranteed Eli had to use the facilities before confronting his friend.

This was familiar ground. Ten years of sharing a bathroom meant someone often had to take care of business while the other was occupied in the shower. Usually it was the other way around. Eli preparing for the day while Alanso relieved himself of some of the beer they'd chugged the night before then stumbled back to bed for another nap.

"Hey." Eli tried not to startle Alanso as he made his way to the toilet. He wondered if Al was imagining his hand holding his dick when he didn't answer immediately.

"Look who it is… Asshole, party of one."

Eli didn't laugh along. The truth stung.

"Didn't hear your alarm go off. Thought you were still sleeping," Alanso finally responded. "Was it the shower that woke you? Sorry."

"Nah." Eli didn't bother with pajamas so it wasn't more than ten seconds before he tugged back the curtain and joined his partner in the shower, despite the sputters of outrage coming from the shorter man's luscious mouth. "I haven't really been to bed. Couldn't manage to doze off with the memory of your mouth on that dude's cock."

"Disgusted you that much, huh?" Alanso glanced away or he might have spotted Eli's hard-on. Even the chilly secondary splash from the shower spray didn't wilt the damn thing.

"Hardly." Eli had done so much harm. He knew one thing that would convince Alanso he was serious about changing the course he'd taken so far. "I think you should be on the lookout. My dad is likely to pay you a visit today."

"Why?" Alanso's breathing grew faster. He ignored the droplets forming on his mocha skin, streaming down his bald head, the powerful cords of his neck and onto his chest. The barbells in his pebbled nipples decorated his pecs, making Eli long to lean forward and lick them like Phil had done the day before.

They stared into each other's eyes. "I told him about us."

"You did *what*?" Alanso might have slipped and cracked his thick skull open if Eli hadn't lunged for him when he jerked. He banded his arm around Alanso's trim waist and tugged him close until they aligned, torso to torso. "Is he going to ask me to leave?"

"Jesus. Would you quit that? He's not your mom. He won't ever abandon you." Eli grabbed Alanso's chin with his free hand and angled the guy's face toward his. "No one thinks less of you for being honest about what you want. I should have done the same. A long time ago. My dad had it right. There's a reason I've never had a girlfriend. I couldn't stand the idea of anyone replacing you in my life. You were right last night when you said I didn't deserve you. But I'm asking you to give me a chance anyway."

"Cobra?" Alanso blinked up at him, crystal drops decorating his long, dark lashes.

"Yeah." He couldn't help but grind his cock on Alanso's hip. The guy was powerful. Stocky and tenacious. He reminded Eli of a pitbull.

The possibility of that much strength focused on him...it had his engine revved in no time.

"As much as I'd kill for what you're offering—"

"What? You're still turning me down?" He drew away far enough to really scrutinize Alanso's expression as best he could in the dim light of the shower area.

"Maybe. I need to ask you something first." He plucked the shower gel from a rack in the corner of the enclosure and lathered up his palms. When he smeared bubbles all over his torso, Eli thought he might choke on his own tongue.

"Spit it out already." Eli couldn't wait much longer. Either to fuck or to know the offer was really off the table for good.

"Not to sound greedy, but..."

"Oh. That." Containing his grin would have been impossible. "Yeah, I plan to live it up, Alanso. I don't know who might be in or how the logistics will work, but, yes, I want what the crew has and I'm willing to do what it takes to sell our Hot Rods on the arrangement."

"*Come mierda!*" His head fell back, knocking into the tile hard enough to alarm Eli. "You're not fucking with me, are you? Please, don't do that to me. Be sure. I can't handle you changing your mind."

"Can't we take this one step at a time?" Eli shuffled closer, insinuating one of his thighs between Alanso's legs. The other trapped him in place. "We don't even know if I'm any good at this. What if you don't like it?"

"Don't think that's going to be a problem." Alanso slithered against him, spreading the soapy foam between their bodies. It felt so good. Hot, slick and soft on top of Alanso's hardness. "But I'm willing to test that theory."

"I hate fighting with you. No one's yelled at me for eating at the drive-thru for the past three days or photobombed my portfolio shots of the last two finished projects or changed the letters on the daily special sign into dirty offers when I wasn't looking. The last couple months have sucked." Eli closed his eyes as he said what he'd been thinking for quite a while. "I've missed you."

"Same goes. So let's make up." Alanso used some of his lady-killer Latin dance moves to undulate his abs and hips against Eli's wet body. Seems they were just as effective on guys. He almost came right then, shooting all over Alanso's thigh.

"Shouldn't that be *kiss* and make up?" Eli leaned in and nipped Alanso's lip before he could lose all semblance of control. But he couldn't stop at just one nibble. He sealed their lips together and devoured the full mouth that seldom stayed this quiet or this serious in his company.

He reached out with one hand, grabbing the bottle of gel. He flipped open the cap and squished a dollop into his palms, then retreated from the temptation of Alanso's kisses before he let the seduction steal all his rationality.

"Turn around."

Alanso obeyed instantly, showing him the array of artwork gracing the bunched muscles of his back, ass, thighs and calves.

"Good idea. I think I'd prefer *fuck* and make up." Alanso braced his hands on the tiles and shoved his ass in Eli's direction.

"Not so fast." Eli smacked that bubble butt hard enough to leave a red imprint of his palm. The spank echoed through their bathroom, tempting him to do it again. And once more. Then he proceeded to massage the soap into Alanso's blushing cheeks before cleaning the rest of his skin.

"Come on, Cobra." He groaned. "I'm not a girl. I don't need that bullshit. I just need you to fuck me already."

"You might not need frills. Maybe I do." Eli squatted to clean Alanso's legs. He rested his cheek in the hollow of Alanso's lower back. He couldn't believe he'd nearly screwed this up. He wouldn't do it again. By the time they were through, Alanso would know he meant this to be about more than physical pleasure.

"Then why don't you let *me* take care of *you*?" Alanso spun around, rinsing himself off in the process. He lifted the gel from Eli and slathered it on his hands. Before Eli could think of some reason to stop him—other than the fact that he didn't intend for the other man to put himself in a one-down position—he'd begun to caress every part of Eli's body.

And all King Cobra could do was concentrate on not crashing to the floor and breaking his neck. Hell no, he planned to stay alive and alert for the fun ahead.

Alanso knelt on the floor and worked his way up from Eli's toes.

Eli held on to Alanso's bald head to keep his balance as he lifted first one leg then the other when instructed. He rubbed Alanso's scalp, enjoying the hell out of how smooth it was. How soft despite the hardness beneath.

"Shit, that feels good Cobra." He leaned into the touch, still cleansing Eli's ankles, then the rest of his legs. When his fist wrapped around Eli's cock, soaping him from root to tip then back again, Eli shivered.

As the water washed away suds, he imagined it also took the guilt and ugliness that had plagued him lately along with it. Alanso did that for him. Made him feel okay with all the blessings he'd been given. Even in the face of his friends' suffering and the total devastation they'd lived through. Sure, he'd lost his mom. But he'd always had his father. And the absolute conviction that his mother had loved him beyond belief.

He swore then and there he'd never let Alanso fear the people special to him could do any less. How could they not value this man? How could he doubt his own worth?

While he debated how to show Alanso what he meant, the man surprised him. The moist heat of his mouth sucking the tip of Eli's dick seemed a million times hotter than the steam billowing around them.

A groan tore from Eli's throat. His fingers curled in Alanso's shoulders, pressing deep into the muscles there. "Wait. Al, wait."

"I'm so fucking tired of delaying." He stopped only long enough to bitch before repeating the gesture, this time taking an extra inch or so of Eli's shaft into his mouth.

If they didn't stop this soon there wouldn't be any going back.

"Just another minute." Eli pressed on Alanso's forehead, moaning when his dick left the paradise it'd only begun to explore. "I have a better idea."

"Let me be the judge of that." Alanso swiped the back of his hand over his lips, making Eli wonder just how much precome had leaked from his cock already. "I thought it was a hell of a plan."

Eli slapped his hand over the shower handle, shutting off the water. He swiped his hands down his body, sluicing rain from his skin before stepping onto the mat and grabbing Alanso's towel. "Here."

He handed the well-used terrycloth to his friend before taking his own off the bar.

They raced to dry themselves.

Eli flipped the towel over his head to squeegee some of the excess wetness from the hair he kept short while Alanso buffed his baldness until it shined. Cobra couldn't help himself. He snapped his towel at Alanso's ass, laughing at his high-maintenance routines. "You know it always looks exactly the same, right?"

"*Come mierda.* So does yours. At least I've got some style." He stood with his legs wide apart, his bulging arms crossed and his cock jutting straight out. "So what the fuck was this great scheme of yours? So far I'm not seeing the perks."

"Last night when I watched you sucking Links' cock..." Eli headed for Alanso's bedroom. He wanted the man to be comfortable.

"Were you even a little jealous?" Alanso hesitated at the threshold. For the first time, he seemed uncertain.

"Hell yes." Eli whipped the plush comforter to the foot of the bed. "It took everything in me not to interrupt and insist you service me instead."

Alanso actually looked relieved. "So let me."

Eli held up his hand, palm out. "You didn't let me finish. Yes, I wondered what it would be like to have you working me over. But I also was curious about what it felt like to you. How did he taste? Did it feel good to have him in your mouth? I always thought women just put up with BJs for the sake of our pleasure, but...it seemed like you were really enjoying yourself."

"I told you. I sucked cock and I liked it. So what the fuck is the hold up?" Alanso stalked closer, staring at Eli's erection, which hung thick and ready against his thigh. "I want to try again. Just to be sure."

"I want to check it out too." Eli applauded himself silently when Alanso's jaw dropped open. "Let's sixty-nine. First guy to come lets the other guy fuck him as a reward."

CHAPTER SEVEN

"You're right. Your idea's better." Alanso took two giant strides and launched himself onto the mattress. His balls bounced as he settled into the comfort of his bed.

Eli grinned above him. Why did Cobra have to be so damn sexy? Tall, lean, tattooed discretely compared to some of the other guys in the shop. His mother's name perched over his heart and the Hot Rods logo arched across his lower belly.

"What're you looking at?" Cobra sank onto the bed, lying with his head toward Alanso's feet.

"Just thinking I'm glad your portrait of Tom is on your back. It'd freak me out to have him staring at me when I do this." Alanso didn't waste any time stuffing Eli's cock into his mouth. He wasn't about to give his friend the opportunity to run.

Coño, he tasted fine. Clean and fresh, without the fake minty flavor of the guy last night. Alanso couldn't have considered a condom with Eli. No more barriers. He knew the guy was clean. His jaw stretched and he psyched himself up to take the full length of Eli's shaft despite the fact that it was several inches longer than Links' or even Alanso's own cock.

Not quite as thick, he found as he measured the girth with his lips and tongue.

Eli groaned. He rolled, grabbing Alanso's ankles—one in each hand. As he rotated, he spread them far apart and pinned them in place. Alanso forgot to suck for a minute as he adjusted to the weight bearing down on him in addition to the wash of warm breath drying his cock and balls.

Sure, the gang hadn't been kidding last night. Catching women had never been difficult. He enjoyed flirting and playing up his accent when it seemed to suit a bar bunny's fantasy of taking a Latin lover. So he'd had a million blowjobs from women who knew their way around a guy's junk. But something about this was different. Whether because the mouth about to service him was male or because it belonged to his best friend, he couldn't say for sure.

He had a guess, though.

With his head tipped back onto his pillows, he let Eli's sac drag along his cheek.

He flicked his tongue over the sensitive head of the Hot Rod's cock when he hesitated. His demand garbled around his mouthful of Eli. "Enough torture."

"Sorry, sorry." Eli came to life. He dropped lower, pressing them together chest to belly. Their height difference meant Eli had to hunch his back a bit, but he managed to get his mouth on Alanso's dick without pulling his own shaft out of Alanso's grasp.

"*Mámamela!*" The directive to suck would have been lost on Eli even if he'd known the term because his cock garbled Alanso's cries.

Still, the motion of Alanso's hips left no room for misinterpretation.

They both knew he was going to lose this battle of wills. He'd dreamed of this too long to keep from pouring his come down Eli's throat. Hell, this was bigger than he'd dared to let himself hope for. Yet he'd like to hold on long enough to qualify as something other than utterly pitiful in his attempt to keep up. In case he couldn't, he didn't want Eli wasting time. He wanted to feel the man's tongue laving him, his lips choking the base of his cock and the stronger suction a guy would impart, knowing just how damn good it felt.

"Is this what you want?" Eli grabbed Alanso's cock. "Feels weird and cool to touch you. It's like doing it to myself except not. I've wondered since that day with the crew if I imagined how hot you were. I didn't."

Eli prevented any coherent response from Alanso when he held the cock still in his grip and licked the head as if it were a lollipop. The smacking of his lips made Alanso sure he tested the taste of his best friend on his tongue.

He had to concentrate on the sequence of engine parts he needed to assemble later today to keep from letting that thought overpower his restraint. Eli hadn't even taken him totally in his mouth yet. Coming so quick wasn't an option. He'd waited too long to waste this opportunity, in case he never got another one like it.

The only way he knew to make Eli quit dallying was to fight fire with fire. He opened his jaw wider, letting Eli's cock embed more fully in his mouth. The angle and his length made his erection a choking hazard, but Alanso didn't let that stop him.

He tried to recall what Phil had done to him the night before and simulated that rippling finger thing with his mouth by hollowing his cheeks and wriggling his tongue all along Eli's length.

"Uhh." Eli grunted and flexed forward. His mouth surrounded Alanso with heat and temptation.

No way was he going to be the only one frantic with desire. He reached up and around Eli's hip to tease the balls threatening to cut off Alanso's air supply where they pressed near to his nose.

"Cheater!" Eli reared back long enough to shout. He shuddered and slurped Alanso's cock farther into his mouth on the return journey.

"Mmm." Alanso didn't have the luxury of retreating with Eli's pelvis trapping his upper body against the bed, but he wouldn't have done it if he could. The vibrations he sent along Eli's shaft seemed to aid his mission.

Then Eli retaliated. He began to bob his head over Alanso's erection, sliding up and down the length with lips and tongue and cheeks.

Alanso's thighs began to quiver as he curled his toes, attempting to stave off the eruption bubbling in his balls. *Just a few more minutes*, he begged himself. A little while longer to experience this bliss. *Please don't let it stop*, he prayed.

With the end near, Alanso took a chance. He let his fingertip wander from the spot he'd discovered behind Eli's balls, which seemed to drive him wild, to the tight pucker of his asshole. The tongue-lashing Ronnie had given Alanso last night had sold him on the merits of playing around back there. He'd never imagined it could feel so fucking good.

But he'd sure as hell like to share that knowledge with Eli.

For two reasons. First being that he liked to please the guy. In bed and out. Second, because he hoped that Eli might be willing to treat Alanso to that riot of sensation from time to time in their future.

The thought that they might have a future at all nearly made Alanso shoot.

He howled as he clamped down on the urge to come. It was too soon to end this euphoria. Like an addict, he wanted to prolong the high.

When his finger nudged the clenched muscle at the opening to Eli's ass, it instinctively tightened. But when he continued to prod and massage, the muscle relaxed, opening to his exploration. Only the tiniest bit of his digit had poked through Eli's resistance when Cobra stiffened above Alanso.

They both froze in absolute amazement as Eli's balls contracted on Alanso's upper lip and Cobra's cock jerked. Eli ripped his mouth from Alanso's cock, probably to protect him as he spasmed. If Alanso didn't know better, he'd think the man was having a seizure.

Eli buried his face between the mattress and Alanso's leg. He growled, moaned and shouted Alanso's name before biting into his thigh. Not hard enough to hurt. Hell no, the pressure almost had Alanso joining the man on top of him in rapture. Almost, but he couldn't quite tip into climax without the escalating pressure of Eli's mouth on his dick.

And that was when he felt it. The first gush of come blasted from Eli's cock.

He prepared himself to drink it all, every last drop.

Stream after stream coated the back of his throat, making him choke a little as he swallowed reflexively. He offered up a silent apology to every woman he'd nearly drowned like this. *Carajo!*

As if Eli could sense his struggle, he attempted to lift up and steal Alanso's treat.

Alanso dug his fingers into Eli's fine ass and trapped him in place. Weak with ecstasy, Cobra couldn't escape and finished emptying those huge *cojones* into Alanso's open, waiting mouth. When he'd finished coming, he unclamped his jaw and kissed the ring he'd indented on Alanso's thigh. Secretly, Alanso hoped it would bruise so he'd have a reminder that this amazing wakeup call hadn't been some kind of dream.

Eli rolled to the side, collapsing on his back.

Alanso flipped around so that they were face to face, their feet propped on his pillows. He brushed the matted spikes of Eli's hair from his forehead. "You okay?"

"I'm pretty sure we can rule out high blood pressure. I'd have had a stroke if I wasn't in good shape there." Eli still gulped like a fish out of water.

A smug smile crept onto Alanso's face. He liked having this effect on his boss.

Then Eli's eyes cleared of the haze of his wicked orgasm. His throat flexed and his Adam's apple bobbed before he said, "Go easy on me."

Alanso flung out his arm, preventing Eli from rolling onto his stomach and presenting his ass. "Cobra. No. We both know I was supposed to lose that game."

"But you didn't." Eli sighed. "You deserve it. Earned a hell of a prize too. I've never felt like that before. Christ, Alanso."

He wrapped his hand around Alanso's neck and brought him close for a kiss. Another shock, as he didn't seem to give a shit that the mouth he tongue-fucked was dressed in his own release. Alanso found himself fighting against the pressure in his balls again.

"Just get me off. Somehow. I don't care. It'll take two strokes of your hand." Alanso grew desperate, writhing in Eli's hold. "Touch me. Please."

"No." Eli separated them. He smiled softly, then kissed Alanso's forehead. "Chicken? I'm about as relaxed as I'm ever going to be. Do it."

He did manage to roll over this time, presenting the full glory of his body to Alanso to do with as he pleased. A man could only argue so much. He didn't claim to be strong. That was what his Hot Rods were for.

Alanso lunged for his nightstand and took out the bottle of lube he used when he jerked off at night, sometimes to the sounds of Eli fucking a woman in the next room. Though, now that he thought about it, he couldn't remember the last time Cobra had brought someone home.

Definitely before the incident with the crew. Why hadn't he noticed that earlier?

"Here." He yanked a pillow from the head of the bed and slapped it against Eli's hip. "Lift up."

When Cobra obeyed, pride and something deeper rushed into Alanso. Eli wouldn't let just anyone do this. His trust and confidence in Alanso spoke volumes without a single word. Al swore to always deserve what Eli gave him.

After making sure Cobra was comfortable, with his limp cock and balls nestled on the pillow, Alanso spread his cheeks. He popped the lid on the lube and drizzled some in the valley of Eli's ass. The guy jumped, cursing under his breath because of the chilly goo.

"It'll warm up in a second." Alanso rubbed it around where it pooled in the dip of Eli's ass, making sure to get him good and slippery. With his other hand, he applied a generous amount to his own cock, working it in with several passes over his steely shaft.

"*Joder*! I've never been this hard." Alanso forced himself to let go. He didn't intend to shut down the party before it had really gotten started.

"Good. Should make this easier." Eli mumbled against the mattress. He'd rested his head on one bent arm. If it weren't for his shoulders betraying his elevated respiration, Alanso might have thought him ready to fall asleep.

"I don't know, Eli." Alanso hesitated. "I'm not sure you can take me. It's a lot just going right into this. You heard Links last night. He said I wasn't ready. That I should play with some toys first."

"He saw me," Eli confessed. "He knew you were mine. And that I'm yours. He told you that so no one would fuck you."

"Seriously?" Something in the neighborhood of Alanso's heart did back flips at the revelation.

"Yeah. There were lights in the bushes near me—"

"Not that part." Alanso rubbed his thumb over Eli's hole, pressing in the slightest bit.

Eli gasped. "Yes. We belong to each other. All of the Hot Rods do. But especially you and me. Always have. Don't you think so too?"

When he glanced over his shoulder, Eli shot him a look full of concern. Alanso couldn't bear to see the arrogant *pendejo* unsure of himself. It just didn't suit.

"Yeah. I do." Alanso leaned forward, blanketing his best friend. He covered the guy he would protect always. The proximity allowed him to lay a kiss, similar to the one he could still feel burning on his forehead, on Eli's cheek. This was so much more than sex to him.

But he was only human. And he needed relief. Badly.

His cock rode the furrow of Eli's ass. Every time the leaking head probed against Eli's entrance, they both groaned. "Last chance, Cobra. I'd gladly take the rest of that blowjob. You have a really talented mouth."

"Thanks, but no thanks. Fuck me, Alanso." Eli barked the command. He growled, "You had your finger in my ass a minute ago—I think that's enough warming up. Just get your cock in there before I do change my mind."

"If you're not sure..."

"That's not what I meant and you know it." Eli rolled his eyes, making Alanso laugh.

"Fine." He spanked the ass on display before him, not feeling the need to be gentle like when he played with a chick. "But for the record, I barely touched you before you went off like a rocket. This is going to be a lot different, *cabrón*."

"Seriously? Your finger felt pretty enormous and deep to me." Eli looked over his shoulder, one eyebrow raised.

Alanso shook his head, giving him yet another chance to change his mind.

He didn't take it.

"Inside me. Now." And though Eli might be the one beneath Alanso, he had all the power. By submitting to this thing between them, he proved just how strong he was and how seriously he took their test. "You're not going to last anyway. I give you five strokes before you pump your load in my ass."

"Keep talking like that and it'll be three." Alanso wrapped his fist around his cock, aimed the tip at Eli's ass and splayed his free hand on his best friend's lower back. He let Eli brace his weight as he shifted forward.

At first he thought it wasn't going to work. No way could the tiny opening accommodate his epic hard-on. He started to retreat.

"Don't you dare," Eli panted. "Try again. Push harder."

"You've got to relax, Cobra." Alanso petted the boss's flank. Rock-hard muscles were drawn tight. At the soothing strokes, they began to loosen. He positioned himself at the gateway to Eli's body once more.

And this time he sank inside, bit by bit.

"*Hijo de puta!*" Alanso shouted. When he paused, Eli seemed to groan louder, so he forged on. Soon the pressure on the head of his cock abated a tiny bit and he plunged in several inches at once. He froze, rubbing Eli's back and mumbling all kinds of Spanish— endearments, curses and reassurances.

He tried desperately to focus on helping his friend accept him in his ass instead of ruminating on losing his male-on-male anal virginity. Otherwise he wouldn't be able to keep from rutting like an animal for the two and a half seconds it would take to explode.

"I'm good now." Eli's promise sounded strained. "Jesus, you're fucking thick. What do you have, a tree trunk back there?"

Alanso laughed. They both moaned at the friction.

"Just little old me." He took the opportunity to smear more lube around the circumference of his erection, impressed at the chubbiness of his cock. It stretched Eli until the ring of muscle was thin and tight where it hugged Alanso.

"Fuck. You." Eli grunted. "No. Better. Fuck me. I don't know how long I can take it this time. Hurry."

"Damn. Sorry, Cobra." Alanso started to retreat. He didn't want to hurt this man. Ever.

"Don't you dare pull out. That'll be worse. Come on. At least let me feel what it's like when it gets good. I want you to come in me. I want to walk around with you inside me today and wonder if anyone else can tell. I hope they can." He sounded like he might be getting horny again.

And no way could Alanso resist that siren song.

He worked his way forward and back until the flat pad of muscle over his pelvis fit tight to Eli's ass. He couldn't stop staring at the juncture of their bodies, where he and Eli became one. Fusing them tighter, he bottomed out.

"That's right. I have all of you, don't I?" Eli already knew the answer to that question. They both did.

"Hell yes." Alanso nuzzled Eli's neck until the man tipped his head, making more room. Al applied his lips to the spot just below his friend's ear and began to suck in time to the rocking of his hips.

"Fuck yeah." Eli didn't try to run, not that he could have. "Leave a mark. Let them all know I'm yours."

Alanso couldn't help himself. He fucked Eli. Not delicately, but as he needed. He rode Cobra while running his hands over the other man's arms, down his sides and through his hair. Never once did he stop feasting on the slightly salty flesh of Cobra's neck. Not when he could feel Eli's heart pounding in the vein there and knew he loved every moment of this as much as Alanso did.

A lifetime of doubt and the fear of rejection flew from his soul. This man would take him, however he was. This friend would never shy away. He accepted Alanso and loved him enough to let him have this.

In fact, it was better than that.

It seemed Eli needed it too. His grunts turned from those of a guy enduring rough treatment to one who reveled in it. The muscles of his ass began to clench rhythmically as he fucked against the pillow beneath him.

When Alanso applied the barest hint of teeth to Eli's neck, he roared. "Oh shit. Al. You're going to make me come again. Fuck. Ahhh."

Alanso might not have believed it, but there was no faking how stiff Eli got beneath him or the way his ass nearly squeezed Alanso's cock in two. He had to ram his hips forward to penetrate the nearly impossible pressure.

Then it relented, becoming intermittent as Eli spilled what little his balls had left to give directly onto Alanso's pillow. The power of that surrender combined with the tailor-made caresses of Eli's body on his.

Alanso shoved up on straight-locked arms, his back arching impossibly as he roared into the quiet morning air. Come jettisoned from his cock, flying up from the very bottom of his balls. It launched inside Eli, splattering as far and deep inside the man as he was capable of sending it.

Still his orgasm continued, lingering until the clamping of his muscles became almost painful and he was sure he had not a drop left to deliver. He tried not to collapse and crush

Eli in the process, but it was no use. Every atom in his body turned to jelly. He counted on his best friend to catch him, cradle him, while he recovered from the storm of passion they'd invoked together.

When his cock softened enough to slip from Eli's body, he shifted, snuggling beside the man who'd trusted him so completely. Sweat adhered their bodies, making him sad as they peeled apart once more. So much for that shower.

"Are you okay?" Alanso traced one of Eli's brows above his closed eyes.

"Mmm." He sounded like more of a pussycat than a poisonous snake at the moment. "Think I'll just take a nap, if you don't mind."

Alanso chuckled. "I could go for one too. Do you need me to go get a cloth or something? Clean you up?"

"Nah. Just want to lay here for a minute. I'm pretty sure you're going to need a new pillow, though." Eli cracked open one eye. It glinted with mischief that was reflected in his crooked grin.

Alanso felt something shift in the space between them. The bond he thought was already indestructible grew and strengthened. From this moment on, he knew they'd never let anything come between them again.

"Thank you." He didn't bother to hide the sheen of tears in his eyes. How could he when Eli had ripped himself open and put his soul on display?

"Anytime." Eli shifted until he could engulf Alanso's hand in his. "Well, except next time. That's my turn to see what had you making all that racket back there."

Alanso coughed. Because he had a pretty good idea what had caused all the noise from beneath him. And he couldn't wait to experience it for himself.

They drifted in utter peace for several minutes.

"Cobra."

"Yeah? What do you need, Alanso?" It sounded as if even those few coherent words took a lot of effort to produce.

"Quit talking to me in your voicemail voice." Al swallowed hard. The sexy rumble made it hard to concentrate.

"What does that even mean?" Eli smiled. He loved it when Alanso made words up.

"You know, like when you recorded your message for the shop. Slow, clear, serious... I admit some of the hang-ups we got at first were me listening to it. It's sexy as hell, and— oh, shit... I just thought of something. It's

Friday, right? Don't you have to be to work in…" He glanced at the clock. "…five minutes? Unless you talked someone else into accepting the tanker delivery this morning."

"Son of a bitch!" Eli slapped his palm on the bed. "You're right. I have to get down there. Unless…"

"I love you and all, but not enough to get out of this bed anytime soon, *cabrón*." When Eli slapped his ass—hard—Alanso full-out laughed for the first time since their trip to help the crew.

Eli leapt from bed and jogged to his room. Alanso rolled onto his side, braced on one arm so he could watch his *lover's* white ass in motion. Never in a million years would he have imagined Cobra would welcome him in there.

Or places even more well guarded.

Like his heart.

CHAPTER EIGHT

Eli kicked back in his office chair. It was the passenger seat of a Ferrari F360 Challenge the guys had salvaged and mounted on a swivel base. They'd surprised him with it for Christmas a few years back. Holden was a genius when it came to reupholstering and the interior work of their restorations. He'd done a great job on this and they used it as part of their portfolio when seducing upscale customers.

Sally had completed the masterpiece by imprinting the back of the headrest with a King Cobra logo and script with some fancy scrollwork he'd never get tired of looking at. In fact, it might have to be his next tattoo. Either that or Alanso's name.

Damn, one day into this crazy turn they'd taken and he was already dreaming like a thirteen-year-old girl. Might as well doodle some hearts on his classic car blotter.

Admitting to himself that detailed office work like the statement reconciliation he'd been attempting was futile, Eli reached for the mail overflowing his inbox.

Bryce managed customer service. He kept urging Eli to hire a business manager. Maybe he had a valid point.

Eli grimaced as the stack of envelopes spilled onto the industrial carpet.

He gathered them up, glancing at the return addresses, until one crisp letter caught his eye. The staid font declared it was from the *National Archives, Records of Immigration and Naturalization Service.*

Was it a coincidence he'd found this today? He'd mailed his inquiry months ago. Did he want to ruin the glow surrounding him and—hopefully—Alanso? He felt like they'd made some progress this morning. Maybe Alanso would finally believe he'd never shake Eli.

Unless something inside the envelope gave him reason to doubt again.

Eli cursed and ripped the letter open. He didn't *have* to share the contents, though he didn't believe in withholding info as a form of protection. Secrets always came back to bite you in the ass. Alanso had a right to know whatever was in this damn envelope. Maybe it was nothing. No news. Records were spotty at best in the government, right?

As he scanned the documents inside, his heart cracked.

It wasn't nothing. It was something.

He knuckled moisture from the corner of his eye. Too many times lately, he'd resorted to that gesture. This was going to suck.

Fortunately the gang had made a lunch run, all but him. He'd told them he'd watch the pumps and deal with any walk-ins while they were hitting the diner downtown. Alanso had offered to stay behind, but neither of them wanted to act differently around the Hot Rods.

Even Tom had joined his "kids". *Shit.* Eli could really use a sounding board right about now. Since it wasn't possible, he did the next best thing.

Abandoning his desk chair with a loving pat, he made his way toward the garage. He couldn't go for a drive, but he could sit in his car and devise a plan for how to break the news. In the garage, his fingers trailed over the high-gloss finish Sally had applied to his Cobra. The new product seemed almost like a thin coat of glass. The deep blue of his classic paint job shone even in the interior space and the contrast of the pearly white racing stripes made him sigh.

He loved this car.

Had since the moment he'd first seen one at a show his dad had taken him to as a kid. He'd sworn then and there he'd have one just like it someday. Once he made up his mind about what he wanted, he didn't change it very often.

This Hot Rod was his for life.

"Cobra?" Sally startled him when she knocked lightly on the passenger window, though he could hear her just fine considering the topless car. "Can I join you?"

"You didn't go with the guys?" He raised a brow at her.

"Nah. Wasn't feeling up to all that commotion. Thought I'd enjoy some peace and quiet for a bit." Her soft admission echoed in the emptiness of the usually bustling space.

Very unlike her to seek out solitude. She'd grown used to activity all around, being raised in a polygamous commune. Lack of company had never been an issue with untold brothers and sisters. When she'd first come to them, she'd often ended up sleeping at the foot of Alanso's bed or on the futon in Cobra's room because being alone frightened her.

Neither of them had minded.

The handle clicked as she pulled it and tucked inside, shutting the door carefully.

"You okay?" Eli scanned her from the Louis Vuitton bandana she tied her hair back with to the shit-kicker boots encasing her guaranteed-to-be-prettily-painted toes. She looked all right. Maybe a little flushed, but sexy as ever. Then again, the tough lady could be sitting there missing a limb and she wouldn't let her pain show. "Need me to take you to the doctor's this afternoon?"

"Oh. Nah." She smiled as she angled herself toward him. Only someone as petite as her would be able to manage folding their legs into that pretzel shape, while keeping her boots off the upholstery, in the tiny enclosure. "I'll live. I'm probably faring better than you, anyway. You only think in your car when you've got a big problem. This baby's for driving, not moping. Please tell me Alanso isn't the trouble. You're not going to dump him, are you?"

"What?" He shook his head. "Hell no. You know me better than that, Sally. Don't you?"

A ghost of sadness crossed her face, making him tilt his head when she answered, "I do. Yes. I'm betting you two are forever. You've been besties since the moment you met. Throw in good sex, and what more could you need? I'm happy for you."

"It doesn't seem like it." It was a statement, not an accusation.

"A little jealous, I guess." She shrugged and looked away. "I'm not getting any younger, Cobra. I want a guy that looks at me like you two drool over each other. Even if you were trying to deny it these past few months."

"I don't think that's going to be a problem, Sally." Eli wished Alanso were here now or that they'd had just a little more time to discuss their long-term game plan. Too many things swirled in his mind. Big things. Things he couldn't afford to fuck up by rushing.

One at a time, he cautioned himself. Slow and steady.

"Yeah. Right." She sniffled.

"You sure you're not coming down with a cold?" Eli lifted up to withdraw a rag from his pocket. He shivered when a slight ache reminded him of how he'd started his morning. "It's clean, I was just going to make sure I didn't get any bug guts on the car last night."

"Thanks." When she accepted the soft cloth, she noticed the paper in his fist. "What've you got there?"

"Bad news."

"Ah, shit. *That's* why you're out here." She wiped her nose daintily then held out her hand. "Well, let me see what's got you all knotted up again. I liked seeing you relaxed this morning. It's been a while."

He nodded, both permission and agreement, before handing her the letter.

Being smart, she read it faster than he had. Then she clutched the paper to her chest and raised the cloth to her face again. Daubing her eyes, she managed to preserve most of her elaborate makeup. He loved seeing what creative work she did on the canvas of her already-gorgeous features each morning.

"His poor mom." She let out a tiny sob.

Eli reached over the gear shifter to hold her hand. He considered dragging her into his seat but didn't want to risk tempting himself. She didn't need him mauling her now. Under the weather and heartbroken weren't conditions conducive to getting it on in a sports car.

Hell, not much was. But he'd make do, if he ever got the chance.

"I have to tell him, right?" He wished there was another option.

"Of course you do." Her wobbling lower lip firmed as she found her legendary determination. "If you don't, I will."

"Will what?"

Eli jumped at the sound of Alanso approaching. The guys must have dropped him off outside so he could walk his bike into the shelter. He'd been upset enough last night to ditch the glowing neon motorcycle at the bottom of the staircase to their apartment.

Not far behind him, the rest of the men marched toward the shop.

In his rearview mirror, Eli spotted them joking around. Bryce punched Holden in the shoulder as wisecracks were doled out like candy at Halloween. Staggered in an uneven line, their forms were impressive. And reassuring. Together they could survive this like so many other devastations before.

He looked to Sally and nodded.

They both climbed from his beloved hot rod to greet the gang.

"Hey, guys. Come in here, would you?" Eli waved them forward and motioned for them to gather around. He was glad to see his dad bringing up the rear. Tom would make sure they didn't go haywire.

"Oh shit. This must be serious. Let me guess…Alanso is horrible at sucking cock and you've decided to go back to women?"

"Kaige!" Sally glared at him.

Tom pretended to plug his ears. But he grinned while he did it.

"Just kidding, *Salome*." The bastard knew she hated her full name. "Everyone in the fucking apartment knows how good Al is. They weren't exactly quiet. Jesus. Could you guys at least have the decency to wait until a respectable hour to make that ruckus? Some of us need our beauty sleep."

"Clearly." Carver looked down his nose at Kaige and plucked one of his dreads from the bunch. "What you're getting ain't working, buddy."

Kaige took a half-hearted swipe at Carver. The bickering could easily have deteriorated into a scuffle if Roman hadn't stepped in and separated them.

"Thanks." Eli swallowed hard. "I'm glad we're all together because what I have to say is going to be difficult. Especially for one of us."

Alanso went white as a sheet, impressive given his darker skin, when Eli looked in his direction.

"Careful, son." Tom put his hand between Alanso's shoulder blades and leveled a serious stare in Eli's direction. "You sure you want an audience for whatever bomb you're about to drop?"

"Yeah. This isn't...personal...about me and Alanso, I mean." He cleared his throat.

"Anything you have to say to me you can say in front of them." Al looked up and down the line of mechanics. "It's not like I won't tell them right after anyway."

Despite Eli's reassurance, the gang seemed on edge as they positioned themselves between Cobra and Alanso.

"I wish you'd all give me a little fucking credit. I'm not going to ditch him. Not today and not ever. Who could walk away from a guy who's your best friend? And more?"

Alanso swallowed hard and nodded. "*Loco,* but I believe you."

"Truth is, Al. No one could leave you."

"Tell that to my mom," he sneered.

"I would." Eli handed Alanso the letter. "I tried, actually. But I'm sorry, Alanso…she passed away."

"What?" He might have stumbled back if Tom hadn't been there to catch him or the rest of the Hot Rods didn't crowd in closer to lend their support.

Mumbles raced through the team as Alanso read the paper, which wobbled like a wheel at the end of a bent axle in his grasp.

"It says she never made it to Cuba." Sally couldn't restrain her tears as she related the official history in much nicer phrasing than the version Alanso digested. Those clinical descriptions would probably be branded into his brain for life.

Eli crossed to him, putting his hands on Alanso's shoulders as he finished discovering the details of an event that was ancient history.

"I guess they didn't believe her when she said she had a child. That she'd left her son at daycare in the morning so she could work. They thought it was an excuse because she couldn't produce any proof. No papers or pictures. How stupid!" Sally swiped the back of her hand under her nose and sidled closer, laying her cheek on Alanso's knotted biceps.

"They took her by van to Florida to deport her." Eli took up when the rest of the Hot Rods looked to him for more information. "Along the way the car broke down. In the middle of the night. They said she was distraught, hysterical, about her baby. The guards didn't listen. And when they took everyone from the vehicle on the side of the road, she ran. In the dark."

"She fled into the highway," Alanso finished reading in a monotone that scared Eli. He crumpled the letter in his fist, then finished on his own. "Was struck and killed instantly by a passing car. Not a drunk driver. Just some poor bastard on his way to third shift. The judge ruled no fault. None but her own."

"Oh God." Tom squeezed Alanso's shoulder from behind. "I'm so sorry, kid."

"Al." Carver reached over and put his palm on their friend's bald head. He rubbed it before stepping aside and letting the other Hot Rods near.

The rest of the guys followed suit, instilling what comfort they could.

Eli stared straight into unfocused eyes. "She never left you, Alanso. Not because she wanted to. All those times, you weren't wrong. She loved you very much. Maybe now you can honor those memories, preserve and cherish them, instead of doubting."

"Don't tell me what to do, *cabrón*. Just because we fucked doesn't mean you know how this feels." He wrenched away from the helping hands on him and punted an oilcan across the garage. It clattered as it rolled before skidding to a stop.

"Fuck you." Eli got right in his face, to hell with the guys attempting to hold him back. "How dare you tell me I don't know what it's like to lose your mother?"

"Eli! Alanso!" Tom cut through their rage in a second. His censure was like a hot knife through butter. "Shut the hell up. Both of you. Neither of your moms would condone this. Haven't you suffered enough?"

"You're right, Tom." Alanso hung his head. "*Lo siento*. I think...I'm going to go for a ride.

I'll be back when I can think straight. I promise."

He wandered toward the exit in a crooked line.

Tom murmured, "Don't let him go. He needs you."

Doubt, confusion, hurt, fear and anger all melted away. Only one thing was important right now. Comforting his mate.

"Alanso, wait," Eli commanded.

And his lover obeyed.

He turned around slowly. A mixture of fury, pain and anxiety radiated from his chocolate eyes, but he returned step by step until he lingered by Eli's side.

"Not alone." Eli opened the door of the Cobra and ushered Alanso inside. "I'll take you anywhere you want. Stay as long as you need. You don't have to grieve by yourself. Trust me, I *do* get it. How bad it hurts. I don't even mind if you need to swipe at me. Anybody. Whatever it takes, I'll have your back. I would never leave you to sort through this on your own. I'd never leave you period. Understand?"

"I think so." Alanso leaned forward, grasping his knees and curling into himself. "Thanks, Cobra. Just motor. I don't care where."

"You got it." He jogged around to the driver's side. Holden shut the passenger door carefully, patting Al's shoulder as Eli tossed his garage keys to Roman. "Lock up tonight, please?"

"Of course." The slap he landed on Eli's ass stung a little, but the pressure was welcome. It gave him something other than the agony in his heart to concentrate on while he buckled his seatbelt.

"We'll see you guys later. Don't worry. Everything will be all right," Roman assured them.

"Come on, Cobra." Alanso rocked now. "Fucking go."

Tom nodded when Eli glanced at his father.

Salome blew them a kiss as they rolled from the garage and weaved down the winding road into the countryside.

CHAPTER NINE

Alanso nearly crashed off his teetering barstool as he leaned forward to flag down the bartender, Ward.

"Don't break your neck, Hot Rod." The guy ambled over as Eli set Alanso to rights on the precarious perch. Swaying himself, it was a tricky operation. "I see you. I'm just not serving you another drink."

"Ah, come on. Plenty of time 'fore last call." He concentrated on not slurring.

"Right. But no way in hell am I risking your girl Sally kicking my ass for poisoning you." He shook his head while running a cloth over beer glasses. "She scares the piss outta me."

"Hey now," Eli chimed in. "Watch yourself."

"I know, I know." Ward grinned. "Nobody messes with your gang."

"Damn straight." His assertion was somewhat less threatening when he belched loud enough to crack Alanso up.

"I'm so glad I'm not going to be you guys tomorrow." Ward smiled as he shook his head. "So what's the occasion, anyway?"

"My mom's dead." Alanso raised his glass, unsure if he would laugh or cry at the dry toast. Didn't matter when the vessel slipped from his fingers and clattered to the bar where it lay rolling in an uneven circle. Luckily, unbroken.

Ward paused. He looked to Cobra, who nodded from where he sat shoulder-to-shoulder with Alanso. "Happened a long time ago. Found out today."

"Shit, man." The apology didn't stop Ward from collecting the empty and refusing to replace it. "I'm sorry to hear that."

"'S okay. Means she didn't walk out on me."

A big, warm hand rested on his shoulder. Eli. "Maybe we'd better text somebody to come get us. A couple somebodies so my car gets home too."

"Sure, Cobra." Alanso patted his pocket. "Don't think I got my phone."

"Here." It took several tries for Eli to jam his hand in his jeans and retrieve his smartphone. "Fuck. Dead battery."

"I could call for you." Ward reached for the bar phone.

"Did I hear that right?" A sultry voice snaked between Cobra and Eli, followed by the woman who'd spoken. It might have been beer goggles talking, but she looked pretty fine to Alanso. She sported a low-cut bedazzled T-shirt, skintight jeans and a pair of sexy cowgirl boots. "Two Hot Rods looking for a ride?"

"Fawn." Eli groaned softly. "Imagine seeing you here."

"The Psycho Ward *is* one of my favorite bars. Maybe yours too after the last time we ran into each other, huh?" She rubbed herself on Alanso's man like she owned him. He would have staked a claim—with a big juicy kiss or maybe a public blowjob—if he'd been able to coordinate his limbs well enough to reach around her fake, balloon-sized tatas.

Well, they were sort of pretty, anyway. He'd like to motorboat them.

"I suppose I have some fond memories here." Eli glanced to Alanso. "But not tonight so much."

"Aww, having a bad day, honey?" She practically climbed into Eli's lap.

Alanso wished he'd thought of that himself. Well, maybe they should go home. It could comfort him to curl up on their enormous sectional couch with Cobra and the rest of the gang.

"More Alanso than me. But yeah." Eli tried to evade her wandering hands and edge toward Alanso.

"Oh boy, that's no good." Her overdramatic pout emphasized her full lips. She wormed her way between them and nestled her rounded booty against Alanso's thigh. "I bet I can help turn things around for you guys."

"Which one of us?" Alanso couldn't believe she'd be as bold as she sounded.

"Well, your boss here can vouch for my skills." She snagged a cherry out of her froufrou drink and twisted the stem into a knot with her tongue. A few chews and she swallowed the fruit, depositing the stem into his empty glass. "Wouldn't mind trying you both on for size."

Ward seemed to have vanished, retreating into the shadows to attend to patrons on the other side of the polished hardwood.

"More than anything, I need to take a whiz right about now." Eli stood and brushed her clinging limbs from his body. She was like a grabby octopus. "You've had more than me, Alanso. Come on."

"We'll be right back." Al grinned at the woman and her sparkly boobies.

"Then maybe you'll give me a few dances before we hit the road?" She gyrated against him. He was only human. She felt good and smelled pretty. Club music acted like kryptonite on his better sense. It worked him up every time.

"Sounds good, Bambi."

"It's *Fawn*, baby." She patted his bald head. "Don't worry, I'll make sure you don't forget after tonight."

Batting her lashes hard enough to start a windstorm in Kansas, she turned and sashayed toward the juke box in the corner.

"Are you crazy?" Eli grabbed Alanso's ear and dragged him to the men's room.

"Nope. But I'm pretty hammered." He laughed as he began to forget about why he'd been so damn depressed. "And I'm about to piss on your sneakers, *maricón*."

"Fucker." Eli shoved him through the swinging door, a begrudging chuckle sneaking around his disapproval. "Don't you dare."

They adopted their stances, whipping their cocks out without any awkwardness. Hell, they'd done this about a million times before. Except tonight Alanso remembered what it was like to taste Cobra's cobra. What it was like to touch him, hear him, feel him.

"*Mierda*! I can't go with a hard-on." He concentrated on the business at hand.

"How the fuck do you have a boner?" Eli looked at him as if he were a freak of nature.

139

"I'm pretty sure we broke some records tonight."

"Eh. Good genes, I guess." He sobered for an instant. "Look, Eli. What's the deal with this girl? Was she hot? Do you like her? Can we...try something?"

"Like what?" Eli tried to stuff his penis in his pants, but the truth was he sported some wood himself, making it difficult to repackage his junk. "Today's been wild enough, hasn't it? Maybe we should call it quits before we do something stupid."

"I'm asking you to do her. With me. I want to know if we can. I didn't like seeing her touch you. But...I still like pussy, Cobra. I'm not, like, completely not wanting chicks anymore." He washed his hands off, then scrubbed some cold water over his face. "*Joder!* This is hard."

"I hear what you're saying." Eli took his time drying his hands. "I agree. I don't know how to say what I want. But, yeah, like the crew. Like the guys. I want both."

"So we're bi, I guess is what I mean." Alanso swallowed hard and looked up at Eli. "Right?"

"Uh, sure." Eli shrugged. "Why do we have to call it something?"

"No reason." He turned to leave.

"Wait." A restraining arm wrapped around his shoulders from behind, tugging him toward the solid warmth of his best friend. "I want you, Alanso. That's not going to change. And yeah, I still feel like messing around with other people. Women. Maybe the Hot Rods if they're into it. Only if you're with me. But...I'm not sure Fawn should be on that list. I'm kind of over sex for the sake of quick relief. It's so much better when it means something. Like this morning."

"I know who I'd like to have most." Sally flashed through Alanso's mind.

"Yeah, me too." Eli rested his forehead on Alanso's baldness.

"But I don't want to fuck that up. This is like starting over. Nothing I knew about dating and how stuff works is true anymore." Alanso hated the tightness in his throat. "I don't have any swag when it comes to this. I need training wheels. Or...whatever Fawn's packing in that skimpy shirt."

Eli chuckled against him. The heat of his breath and the dampness of his lips weren't helping the situation in Alanso's pants.

"Okay, what you're saying makes sense. Kind of." Eli shook his head. "But I don't think tonight's the night. It's not smart. We're wasted. Let's consider this when our brains dry out."

"Mmm-hmm," Alanso agreed. "Fine. Right, as usual. But can we at least dance some of this off so I'm not dying tomorrow?"

"I'm not so great at that. Not like you with those damn hips." A groan fell from Eli's throat.

"You weren't complaining 'bout my hip action this morning, *amigo*." He trotted toward the door before Eli could retaliate. "Come on. You're drunk enough not to care what you look like."

"Great. Real comforting. Asshole," Eli grumbled, but followed.

"Maybe later you can play with it. If you practice the motion of the ocean." Alanso didn't wait for a response. He strode over to the dance floor, undid a few buttons on his shirt, and showed off his chest and abs as he undulated to the beat of Don Omar's "Taboo".

When he curled his fingers to beckon Fawn or maybe Eli, who stood behind her, they both answered his call.

***

A couple hours later, Eli believed he was much more grounded. The loopy daze and comforting numbness had worn off. In fact, some of him felt like he'd gotten internal road rash. He couldn't wait to faceplant into his bed. Or maybe Alanso's. Those damn sheets had been as luxurious as they looked.

"You boys going to invite me in for a drink?" Their courtesy cab driver licked her red lips and tossed her hair as she parked in front of Hot Rods.

"I don't think we're up for that tonight, Fawn." Eli climbed from the car. "Sorry we dragged you out of your way, if that's what you expected. Go ahead and pull up to the pump. I'll fill your tank for your trouble."

"I'd rather a tour of your shop instead." She winked at him. "I have a thing for big engines, you know?"

Alanso caught his gaze and shrugged. What was five more minutes before getting upstairs to the rest of the guys, Sally and bed? Ugh. It seemed like a lot, but what could he say? She *had* carted their lame asses home.

"Sure." He opened her door and handed her out. Mostly so she wouldn't bust her ass in those crazy cowgirl boots. Last thing they needed was a lawsuit.

Of course she took the opportunity to falter, snugging up tight to his side and encircling his waist. Though he knew it was just his hormones talking, Eli couldn't deny she felt nice. Toned, yet soft in all the right places.

Maybe he was being too rash. He'd had her once before. At least, he'd come in her mouth after a behind-the-bar blowjob. When he'd offered to return the favor, she giggled and said she'd take a rain check. He'd assumed she just liked the power of reducing a guy to begging. Now he wondered if she expected him to make good on his debt.

Alanso glanced over at him and mouthed, *Please?*

The uncertainty mirrored in his friend's warm gaze stabbed Eli hard in the gut. If this would ease his worry and erase some of the stress of the day, instead of adding more, who was he to make that call for them both?

"Shit." Eli remembered too late that he'd tossed his keys to Roman. Double shit when he grabbed the handle, tested it and the heavy metal swung open. "It's impossible to find good help these days."

He made a mental note to follow up on security measures in the morning, then held the door for their guest. When Alanso passed, Eli whispered, "You're on. Let's see what we can do. Together. Practice for when it actually counts."

Alanso winked and trailed his hand over the bulge in the crotch of Eli's jeans. "My turn."

CHAPTER TEN

Salome twirled her paintbrush, then dabbed it in the purple oils she'd mixed up to exactly the right hue on her palette. She swirled the bristles through the paint then began to stroke it onto her canvas. Which wasn't actually a canvas at all. Nor was it a car for once.

The memorial rock she decorated mimicked the one that held a place of honor in Tom's memory garden. Surrounded by wildflowers, it had become a spot for all of them to go to contemplate what they'd lost and the home they'd found.

Alanso should have a marker for his mother. Something to remind him of the adoration his heart had harbored since he was a little boy. He'd loved the woman who hadn't abandoned him by choice. Now maybe he could give himself permission to admit it. At least Sally hoped he'd work up to that stage eventually.

Art was the only thing that could calm her when her mind raced along dangerous curves. She couldn't put the brakes on imagining all the horrible reasons the pair of Hot Rods hadn't answered her calls. Or Tom's, for that matter.

Where had they gone? Were they safe? Was Alanso okay?

She switched brushes and added an elaborate swirl of contrasting green behind his mother's name.

And then she heard it. The roar of an engine. It didn't sound like Eli's Cobra, but no one else would pull up at this hour. Maybe they'd taken a taxi.

"Oh thank God." She finished the section she worked on, unwilling to risk a color mismatch in the morning when it'd cost her just a few minutes to complete the design. She was nothing if not a perfectionist.

Besides, it'd take a bit for the guys to pay the driver and collect themselves. Especially if at least one of them had been drinking. Still, why hadn't they called her for a ride?

Her nerves got the better of her.

Cans rattled as she slopped thinner into them then dumped in her brushes. A few more details and she'd be set to advance. Ready to open her arms to Alanso, she covered the switch with her fingers. About to shut the light to her workspace off, she prepared to welcome him home. Gently, with warmth and empathetic kindness. In some ways, she'd lost her entire family too.

And that's when she heard a gasp.

"I knew you boys would change your minds." Obnoxious fake giggling followed.

They didn't! They wouldn't!

Sally cracked open the door to her studio and saw... Yes, they surely would.

Artificial platinum blonde hair whipped around as the object of their combined attention squirmed onto the hood of the Fisher restoration they'd just finished today.

Sally couldn't believe they'd brought some skank to the garage. Even worse, Eli let that bitch make an ass print on the perfect paint job she'd slaved over for a full day. Those fucking pricks!

She tried to drum up more anger. But the truth was, it hurt.

Watching them together last night had bruised her heart. She wanted so badly for them to reach out and enclose her in their circle of desire, trust and love. But they hadn't. The only thing that had kept her spirits lifted was the stupid idea that maybe they were taking things slow. Finding their way.

But, it looked more like despite their constant flattery, she just wasn't their type.

Her boobs couldn't compare to that fake rack. For Christ's sake, those things didn't even budge when Eli yanked up his guest's shirt, rocking their toy several inches higher on the hood of the candy apple red '57 Thunderbird.

Even worse, Sally was trapped.

If she broke from her hiding spot behind the cracked open door to the painting booth, they'd spot her instantly. Enduring the awkwardness of that encounter was not something she wanted to add to the list of horrible experiences she'd been subjected to in the past twenty-four hours.

Crying was not an option. She'd done too much of that over these jerks already. Couldn't they see how much she loved them? Didn't it matter that she'd worship them and only them—well, just the Hot Rods, at least— instead of half of Middletown? And she wouldn't be stingy with her affection as soon she got off.

Apparently it didn't bother them to drive a model with sky-high mileage.

Not if the way they unwrapped the woman's tits was any indication.

Hell, it might as well have been Christmas. The lacey bra, which Sally begrudgingly admitted was very pretty and ultra feminine, was like some fancy paper removed with delicate swipes by the pair of dirt bags.

She liked her own style, but it blended in enough edge that it intimidated some guys.

Somehow, she'd thought her Hot Rods were different.

Guess not.

Each man took up residence on one side of the airhead. Alanso moaned, *Fawn*, before he latched on to the hardened tip of her nipple. Seriously? Big, dumb prey? She did have doe eyes that were rolling back as the guys got her up to speed.

Yet Sally couldn't back away, close her eyes or even blink. Because she'd imagined a similar scenario so many times, she couldn't believe that what she saw was real and not a figment of her envious imagination.

Eli reached up to knead the mound Alanso suckled. He plumped it for his best friend and helped the gorgeous bald man feast until he got his fill. Hungry, he licked, nipped and sucked some more.

While the engine man concentrated on laving Fawn's breast, Eli turned his attention to Alanso.

He stroked one hand up the guy's back, inspiring a shiver so intense Sally caught it from her station. When Cobra reached chest height, he snaked around and began to undo the buttons of Alanso's shirt. Some must have already hung loose as it didn't take long before Eli peeled the soft chambray from his best friend.

He paused when Alanso's wrists became entangled in the fabric. Pinned behind him, the shorter of the two didn't struggle to get free. In fact, he seemed to linger in the confines of his soft prison, implicitly trusting Eli to drive.

Shaping the result of their actions into pleasure greater than the two of them could have experienced alone seemed effortless for their boss. He used his thumb beneath Alanso's jaw to tip his head back. Then Eli took advantage of his friend's prone position to swoop in and seal his lips over the parted mouth of the panting engine master.

Instead of enjoying the show, as Sally would—hell, as she *did*—good ol' Fawn began to whine. "I thought you two were into me. Not each other."

"Why can't it be both?" Alanso hesitated.

If that bitch hurt him or made him timid about expressing his desire for Eli, nothing could hold Sally inside her bay. She'd jab a paintbrush in the woman's eye and beat her with her own boot.

"I like to be the center of attention." She pouted.

"Sorry," Alanso nuzzled her breasts, insinuating his face into her cleavage. "Got carried away there. Good point. Eli, we have to always remember to not let our girl feel left out."

The endearment from him nearly made Sally sick.

Her knees trembled and her stomach flipped.

Why couldn't she have been the one to satisfy them?

Fawn made a grab for Alanso, but he resisted kissing her on the lips. "Sorry, I'm not big into that."

Eli looked at him like he was full of shit. Hell, hadn't they just been about to suck face for a solid half-hour at least? It'd sure seemed like it from here. Sally could have watched that all day, never mind for a few minutes.

This girl was dumber than she looked. And that was saying something.

"Fine then." She huffed. "Let's jump right in. Somebody take their damn pants off. Mine too."

Eli didn't hesitate or bother to argue. He reached down and unbuttoned her jeans, then peeled them over her hips. She shed the denim like a snakeskin, making Sally realize how unappealing her own baggy work cargos and paint-slathered coveralls were compared to something like...that.

Once Fawn's pants drooped to her ankles, she kicked them off with a dainty flick, leaving her boots in place. Sally cringed when the bitch propped those clunky heels on the bumper. Apparently Alanso had his limits too. He removed the shoes with a swipe of his hand over each foot and tossed them a safe distance from the polished automobile.

Seduction had no place here. The guys operated in sync, with efficient yet brusque movements. They had a goal. It was right there between Fawn's thin, spray-tanned-to-the-point-of-oompa-loompa-orange thighs.

She must have decided not to wait any longer and wriggled out of her skimpy ass-floss, flinging the loop of lace into a toolbox nearby. Without wasting any time, she dipped her fingers onto the heart-shaped landing strip of trimmed hair above her pussy and played boldly with herself.

Sally had to give the girl props on that at least. She would have been a lot more shy. *Note to self: Maybe guys like confidence in bed.* Holding her own in the shop was easy. In sexual situations, less simple. Sometimes she still panicked at that look in a guy's eyes. The one that proclaimed he was about to take away her control...

Swallowing hard cleared the knot from her throat.

The guys helped too.

They got naked in a hurry.

Salome drooled. For a moment she erased Fawn and the ghosts of her past from her mental scenery. Actually, more like all she could see were the two Hot Rods. Sure, she'd drank in the sight of them shirtless a bazillion times as they strutted around the garage covered in grease and sweat. Or spied them in their shorts, grazing the snack cabinet of their shared apartment in the middle of the night.

She couldn't even count how often she'd spotted their bare assess when they'd gone through that mooning phase in their early twenties. Oh, those were the good old days. But it'd been a while and the guys had filled out some. More of the artwork she'd approved, and even drafted in some cases, decorated their skin.

To her, they were masterpieces.

The scar on Eli's elbow where he'd thrown his arm in front of a falling piece of sheet metal to protect Holden made her want to kiss it.

"You first." Eli graciously gestured toward the willing woman laid out for their enjoyment. He took himself in hand. It surprised her to see he wasn't entirely hard. Didn't he want to fuck this bar babe? Or maybe they'd drunk too much to perform up to their usual standards.

They'd been gone forever. And she had no doubt of their prowess. None of them were especially discreet, either with accounts of licentious nights or with the vocalizations of their pleasure when they brought women home. She thought she'd gotten used to it.

Clearly not.

Especially when they'd finally explained what had happened with the crew and how all her dearest fantasies could actually be within grasp. Right before they'd shattered her hopes.

Alanso looked to Cobra, then shook his head. "Be right back."

Sally gasped when he turned toward her hiding spot. He jogged in her direction, his erection swaying in time to the fluid grace of his strides. *Oh shit!*

He tipped his head at the light streaming from her studio. Then shrugged and veered to the right. Into the supply closet.

What the fuck?

Several rapid heartbeats later, he emerged with something shiny in his fist. Condoms. The guys kept an emergency ration on the shelf by the first-aid kit. She had often tried not to notice how quickly the level dropped.

Was it because of her upbringing that she got horned-up by the community of sexy men surrounding her each day? That secret fear had kept her from expressing her misplaced curiosity for years.

Alanso handed the packets to Eli, who ripped one open.

Wetness gathered in her decidedly not ass-floss panties when Cobra grasped his partner's hips, rotated the guy toward him, then sheathed his cock with expert handling. He gave Alanso's hard-on a few test pulls before slapping his partner's ass and encouraging him to, "Go get her."

Fawn wrinkled her nose at the display that warmed Sally's heart, along with regions slightly farther south.

Alanso stepped between the woman's knees and tugged her low enough to align her pussy with the tip of his cock. His jerky motions and the way he kept glancing at Eli emphasized the impact of today's revelations on the man. He was never less than smooth.

"Do it," Cobra encouraged him. "You wanted to know what it would be like."

"It's not the same as I thought," he murmured.

Eli stepped behind Alanso, blocking some of Sally's fantastic view. Well, replacing it with a different manscape. He wrapped his lover in his arms and held on for a moment before sliding his hands lower to the still-firm cock and heavy balls at the apex of Alanso's thighs.

The way he touched his friend, with authority and a sense of how much pressure was enough, awed her. So different than the care she'd taken with the men she'd tried on for size.

Cobra positioned Alanso's cock so that the tip insinuated itself in Fawn's pussy.

When the woman's eyelids fluttered closed and she mewled, Eli swooped in close. He whispered things intended for Alanso's ears only. If the woman a dick's length away couldn't interpret the swish of sound, Sally certainly had no chance. But whatever coaching Eli did seemed to slam Alanso into gear.

Spanish began to flow from his lips. She loved to hear him speak it. He'd taught her enough that they could piss off the rest of the Hot Rods by having coded conversations. But now it was too fast, too broken for her to catch more than a lot of curses.

Ones he meant in a good way, apparently.

He tipped forward and began to fuck. His powerful thighs flexed as he bent then straightened. The quasi-squat drove him deeper into Fawn with each thrust. Sally was surprised to see he'd closed his eyes when the bounty of their catch's chest loomed so near.

Instead, he seemed more infatuated with the pressure of Eli's now-stiff cock riding the crack of his ass.

"Are you going to do me, Cobra?" He glanced over his shoulder.

"What?" Fawn roused from the hood. She levered up onto her shoulders. "Are you guys gay or what? I never heard any rumors about that. Lots of other crazy stuff, but never that."

Holy shit. Was she enjoying the lavish attention of these two dream guys or not?

Sally wanted to march out there and slap the cunt. Her voice didn't even hold a hint of smoke. She'd snapped from her artificial moans the instant the guys didn't grant her their full interest. Fawn might have even bigger issues than Salome.

Huh.

Anger crept up inside her, burning her chest, neck and cheeks. The Hot Rods were wasting their effort on this ungrateful cow. Sally would have taken their affection and magnified it. She would have reflected it back, brighter and more focused than they shined it on her.

"Do you want him to fuck you or not?" Eli growled.

"Yeah, yeah." Fawn collapsed onto the hood again, her hair billowing out from beneath her shoulders. "Harder. Give it to me."

Sally rolled her eyes.

With Fawn's attention diverted, Eli continued his subtle flexing. His ass cheeks bunched then relaxed, gliding his cock through the valley of Alanso's crack as the man began to pick up steam. At the end of the day, it was a physical reaction, especially with Eli triggering illicit pleasure from behind.

Had they done it yet? Had they tried fucking?

It sure had sounded like it this morning. But she knew the guys well enough to know their voices. Even when they turned into guttural shouts and groans.

It had been Eli making the most noise.

What if he'd let Alanso take him?

Sally couldn't help it. She slipped her fingers into the waistband of her pants, rubbing the knot of her engorged clit. Ignoring Fawn, she concentrated on the intersection of Eli's and Alanso's bodies. If Eli hadn't taken him yet...did that mean...

Was Alanso still an anal virgin?

Was Cobra teasing him mercilessly?

It sure would explain the way Al threw his head back, so it rested on Eli's shoulder and the cording of his neck as he pumped his cock deeper, harder, faster into Fawn.

"Now we're talking." She scratched her fire-engine-nails down Alanso's chest, probably leaving a mark. When she made like she'd repeat the gesture, Eli removed her hands.

Clearly, no one had the right to claim Alanso. No one other than him.

Sally wished she could be appended to that list.

She rubbed circles over her pussy as Eli shuffled closer, nestling his dick against Alanso's ass tighter so the man had to be imagining what it would feel like to be stretched wide and welcoming his boss deep.

Hell, Sally was. Wondering both what it would be like to see Alanso taken and to experience the rush herself as a third in their exchange. A gasp left her lips when the idea alone triggered a clenching of her internal muscles. No one seemed to notice.

She bit the inside of her cheek to keep quiet.

Alanso made no such effort.

He grunted so loud the guys upstairs probably heard. Except they'd assume he was fucking Eli down here, not some cheap date.

Okay, so part of her knew she was being unfair to Fawn. The woman wasn't doing anything wrong. But it wasn't like they even cared for her. Not like the girls they sometimes laughed with or found interesting for a week or two. Yet she didn't seem to care.

If Sally were to be offered the chance to switch places with the woman right now, she wasn't sure she'd do it. She had to have both. Their carnal hunger *and* their affection. Neither of which seemed likely.

So instead she focused on what real caring she could see.

Eli continued to love Alanso from behind. Gentle, steady and thorough—he combined his subtle rocking with the counterpoint of Alanso's thrusting hips. Together they worked the system to deliver what they both needed.

In fact, Eli began to flush. His cheeks grew ruddy, like they were when he came in from a long run. His respiration emulated those early-morning post-workouts too. His chest met Alanso's back on each ragged inhalation. The contact seemed to rev them both higher.

Fawn began to chant, "I'm close."

The men let her derive whatever pleasure she could from their presence, but they seemed intent on each other too. More so, if Sally was being honest. Poor Fawn. Eli's hands migrated to Alanso's waist and gripped him tight. The white-knuckled clasp proclaimed his desperation and shot sparkles of arousal through Sally's veins as if champagne bubbled there instead of blood.

She wanted to witness Cobra surrender his legendary control.

Just this once.

Please.

Alanso held on with Herculean effort. His jaw clenched as he kept fucking and fucking—both Fawn when he drove forward and Eli when he put it in reverse. She would have sworn he did it for Cobra. If it weren't for his best friend, he'd have come already and gotten his quick relief. At least his misery seemed to have morphed into something easier to handle for the moment.

A few more passes of Alanso's toned ass over the full-length of Eli's impressive hard-on and Sally couldn't believe her eyes. Cobra stiffened. He dipped his head enough to bite into the nape of Alanso's neck like a dog securing its mate.

The mouthful of muscle also kept him from shouting and alerting Fawn to their game. With her eyes closed, absorbing the impact of Alanso's ramming hips, the woman on the car missed everything special about the encounter.

From this angle, Sally had all the good stuff to herself.

She beamed. Her fingers moved faster, tracing her slit and playing with her clit. She knew what was coming and she had to share it with them. For tonight only. And every night after in her dreams. Because she would never be able to wipe this from her memory.

Recalling the bond between the two men would be enough to fill her fantasies forever.

Her eyes dried out as she refused to blink, afraid to miss an instant or let her arousal keep from building along with theirs. She didn't want to miss her chance.

No need to worry.

The instant Eli erupted, splattering Alanso's lower back with a puddle of come, she mimicked him. Her body launched into an epic orgasm that seemed to match his in intensity. Every time he spasmed, launching another shot of cream across Alanso's glistening skin, she clenched too.

Orgasm exploded through her, making her see stars. She leaned against the doorjamb to stay upright and covered her mouth with her free hand to keep from alerting them to her presence. Eli's pleasure seemed to go on as long as hers did.

The amount of semen he painted across Alanso impressed her.

Until she began to float down from the high and realized she'd crashed their party.

Horror infiltrated her relief. Guilt ate at her consciousness. Fully engrossed in their play, they wouldn't notice her if she stuck to the shadows she bet. Hell, they hadn't spotted her as more than a friend in the decade they'd lived together. She might as well be invisible.

Sally withdrew her hand, her body still humming. She took a deep breath, then snuck from her hideout, clinging close to the wall as she fled the scene of her crimes. It would have been impossible to stand there and watch them finish. To witness them give everything she wanted to some animal who didn't adore them for anything more than the size of their cocks or their handsome faces or the attention they'd give in exchange for basic relief.

Cool night air splashed her face and doused some of the flames they'd inspired. Ice froze her heart. The door might have made some noise as it shut behind her but she figured they wouldn't notice just now. When she raced upstairs, she didn't stop to answer the guys who called to her from the couch, where they watched some action flick.

The sound of explosions covered her sobs.

It also masked the echoes of her name on Alanso's lips as he overflowed the garage with his cries of completion, royally pissing off Fawn.

Even if it weren't for the sound effects of the Hot Rods entertainment, the shattering of Sally's heart deafened her.

CHAPTER ELEVEN

"I'm so glad your kids get you up at the asscrack of dawn." Alanso smiled and waved to the babies Joe and Mike held. "Plus the time difference between us helps."

"Why aren't you guys in bed yet?" Morgan wanted to know. She sat between the men and alternated entertaining each of their children. "Rough night?"

"You could say that. We fucked up." Eli let his head fall back and thump into the dark wood of Alanso's bed.

"No kidding." Joe laughed. "You should have done this months ago."

"Well, yeah, there's that. Mistake *número uno*." Alanso shook his head. They sat shoulder to shoulder in his room, videochatting with various members of the crew.

This was pretty cool. To see them and talk to them. It made Eli feel less far away from his distant family and the guys who'd become extended members by default.

No wonder Alanso had been addicted to this thing lately. He always had been the smarter of them when it came to people. Emotions.

Hopefully he could figure out a way to go forward. They needed direction.

"Don't let them bully you." Kate popped onto the screen as she snuggled into her husband's grasp. Mike sat with Joe, not unlike Alanso and Eli. Except their warmth and happiness was undeniable. The two little babies the muscular guys held attested to the strength of their love and its ability to grow.

Nathan and Abby cooed at each other, their miniature hands seeking their pal with clumsy swipes. Alanso noticed too. "Damn, they're BFFs already, aren't they?"

Kate giggled as she finger-combed Abby's hair. "Yeah. If we take one out of the room the other will bawl until we bring them back together."

"It's not pretty." The wry grin on Joe's face declared he didn't mind so much. "They're assuming control over here. Not even a year old and they have every last one of their aunts and uncles wrapped around their fingers."

Eli wiggled his own fingers when Nathan glanced his way. He smiled at the wide-eyed fascination in the little guy's gaze. "This one included."

"Then maybe you'll come see him in person sometime soon?" Morgan fit just right in the gap between her husband and Mike.

"If I can find the time. Business is doing great. Lots of work." Pride filled him. Even in tough times for luxuries, their clientele never slimmed. They did good work and people knew it. Customers came from several counties away to have Hot Rods attend to their babies.

Only the best.

"I was kind of wondering." Mike hesitated. As the foreman of the crew, he and Eli had always had plenty in common. "Wasn't sure about that since you could spare Mustang Sally for a few weeks."

"What?" Eli cocked his head.

"Uh-oh." Joe poked his crewmate in the side. "I don't think she's told him about her vacation yet."

"Look, King Cobra." Morgan always loved to use their nicknames. "She said she had time coming and she never gets to hang out with other women. Please don't harass her. Let us take her shopping and spoil her and...talk to her."

"What's all this about?" Alanso leaned in closer, scrutinizing their expressions. "When did she tell you she was coming?"

"Honestly, *we* told *her*." Kate sat up straighter, daring them to say one word. "Something's wrong. It's obvious. Just when we've got you two straightened out. Now Sally."

"What the hell are you talking about?" Eli didn't like the unease infiltrating his gut.

"She called earlier." Morgan looked at something off screen so she didn't have to meet their horrified stares. "It was obvious she was upset. She didn't say why, but I can guess."

"It's our fault." Alanso sagged. "Do you think she's grossed out by me and Eli? Will it bother her to live with us now?"

"I think you're *still* fucking this up," Mike barked. He didn't often lose his temper. The babies fussed a little and he melted immediately. He kissed Abby on the forehead and hugged her tight to his chest.

"Stop talking in code." Eli couldn't take much more of this.

"I don't think Sally's offended by your relationship. I think she's crushed you left her out." Kate spoke softer, "I know you didn't do it on purpose but something...somehow..."

"It was very obvious," Morgan confirmed her best friend's observation. "She's had her heart broken."

"Then let's go find her. Talk to her. Cobra, we can't let her leave. Not after tonight—"

"Fuck!"

"*Joder!*"

They cursed simultaneously, if in two different languages.

"It didn't take long for you to start thinking in each other's brains." Mike laughed. "But maybe you want to clue us in."

"We sort of hooked up with a chick in the garage earlier." Alanso scrubbed his hand over his face.

"Do you think...could she have seen us?" Eli had never felt so sick—or so embarrassed—in his life.

"*Come mierda.* I saw the light on in her studio, but I thought she'd just forgotten to turn it off again like usual." Alanso froze.

"Yep, I'd say there's a pretty good chance." Joe grimaced. "You idiots. Why? Why did you waste your time when you knew what you really needed?"

"Because I was afraid of fucking it up." Alanso didn't sound like he felt any better than Eli did. "I wanted to be sure before we approached her."

"And I'm still working my way through this." Eli waved his finger between Alanso and himself. "My dad said something about breaking up the band. Wondered which one of us would fuck up Hot Rods first. Not in so many words, but... Yeah, it made me worry."

"I understand the responsibility you feel." Mike didn't try to bullshit them about everything at risk. "But you aren't helping anyone by putting off the inevitable. You're only causing a lot of drama and delaying the outcome. Man up, Eli. Take your Hot Rods to the next level."

He closed his eyes.

When he opened them again, he nodded. Alanso smiled and knocked his shoulder into Eli's chest, causing the garage owner to show his hand. "Okay, then I guess we'd better go find our girl. Alanso took some notes while we were...busy...earlier. Maybe we could put them to good use."

"Uhhh." Kate looked to her husband, who nodded. "Sally's not home. She's sort of on her way here."

"What?" Right now?" Eli bounded from bed, uncaring that the camera now only caught him pacing. "When she's upset? In the dark? Jesus. It's a five-hour drive!"

Alanso buried his head in his hands, leaving his bald scalp to reflect the soft lamplight. He murmured, "She left?"

"I'm not happy about her hasty retreat either." Mike grimaced. "I tried to convince her to wait until morning—well, later morning—but she wouldn't hear of it. Honestly, though, she's got her hands-free unit hooked up and Kayla's in the other room keeping her company on the road."

"Thank God for Bryce and those new additions he's been testing out." Eli unwound just a tiny bit. "I don't like it, but I guess there's nothing I can do."

"You could get your plan together. Talk to Alanso. Talk to the rest of the guys. Figure out what you need so that when she comes home, you're ready." Mike's direct tone convinced Eli he'd thought about the solution for a while. "Don't chase her, Cobra. She'll be safe here. Let our women talk to her. Convince her of the benefits so you can plead your case once she's cooled off and calmed down. It might do you some good to be without her for a bit. Maybe then you'll get your priorities straight. These people are not going to hang around forever. Not even for you. If you don't love them back—"

"I do!" Eli pounded his fist into his palm.

"All right, then." Mike held his hand out. "Take the time you wanted. You've got it now. Do this right. I'm afraid it's going to be your last shot."

"You text me the moment she walks her pretty ass through that door," Eli snarled.

"Want me to spank her for you?" Joe wiggled his eyebrows.

"Hey!" Morgan slapped her husband lightly on the shoulder. "Isn't it enough that you have four guys and four women of your own to play with?"

"Just offering a public service." He bussed his wife's cheek. "I can't handle anymore anyway. I pity the Hot Rods. That's a tall order."

The crewmembers laughed.

"I want to be you when I grow up," Alanso said softly.

"You're going to get there, honey. It's complicated." Morgan blew him a kiss. "Just keep your King Cobra in line and you'll be on your way."

"Promise?" He couldn't help but smile at the pretty woman who'd tamed Eli's cousin.

"Cross my heart." She did.

"Take care of Sally." Alanso rubbed his head. "I love her."

"We know." Kate smiled back at him. "And she's obviously got feelings for you. Strong ones. Or she wouldn't be running so hard."

"I hope we haven't destroyed that." Eli groaned. "Not when we were so close."

"Don't get ahead of yourselves." The voice of reason, in the form of a construction foreman, warned them. "In fact, it seems like you've had one hell of a day. Why not hit the hay? If Mustang Sally isn't here in the next three hours and forty-two minutes or she gets disconnected from Kayla, I'll call you back. I swear."

Alanso seemed to melt into the pile of pillows on his bed. "You might have another great idea there."

"Please, don't make his head any bigger." Kate rolled her eyes. "Sleep well, guys. And Alanso, I'm so sorry to hear about your mother."

He let his lids sink and nodded. Eli climbed under the blankets beside him and gathered him to his chest. "You're right, it has been a long one. Thank you. For everything."

"Anytime. Goodnight boys," Morgan said with a smile.

Joe, Mike and Kate waved just before the screen went black.

Eli closed the laptop and set it on the nightstand before curling up behind Alanso. "We'll make this right. I'll fix it for us, Alanso."

"We'll do it together, Cobra."

"Even better." Eli smiled and laid his head beside his best friend's on their shared pillow. The rumble from the living room entertainment center soothed him as he thought of the rest of the Hot Rods nearby.

All but one.

CHAPTER TWELVE

"Eli." The soft call rang through the darkness. Though the barest hint of salmon had begun to brighten the window, the man in Eli's arms was still draped in shadows.

"Yeah." He wrapped Alanso tighter, drawing him flush to his chest. They'd ended up lying on their sides, Eli behind his head engine tuner. Holding on to the other man helped ease his anxiety over Sally's safety just a little. More than two hours remained on the countdown clock to full-out panic.

"I can't sleep, Cobra."

"Me either." He sighed. "I keep thinking of Salome and how unworth it tonight was."

"*Lo siento*. This is all my fault. I pressured you. And I have to be honest." Alanso held his breath, then let it out slowly. "That sucked donkey dick."

"Mmm. Yep." A snort caused Eli's head to bounce on Alanso's shoulder as he tucked around the shorter man. He rubbed up and down Alanso's calf with his foot. The hair and hardness there felt so different from the women he'd slept with, it fascinated him. "It did. The worst sex I've had since my first time with Mary Beth Cole. I swear, I thought she was going to bleed to death after I popped her cherry. Tonight was so awful—you've ruined me for flings. But I'm responsible too. I've been in denial for months. You wouldn't have looked for a surrogate if I'd just given in to what we really lusted for in the first place."

"I guess." Alanso was too polite to admit the truth.

"I was trying to keep us from jacking up our relationship with the Hot Rods, yet in the end, that's exactly what I forced us into doing. Damn it." Eli deliberately relaxed each grouping of muscles in his body when Alanso began to caress his forearm, alerting him to how tense he'd become.

"Plus, I'm still horny." Alanso picked his head up just to thump it onto the pillow again. His bald skull left a dent in the feathers. "That bullshit screw didn't help at all. Especially when I can't stop thinking of Mustang Sally watching us. I know it's messed up but that kind of turns me on. A helluva lot more than *Bambi* ever could have."

"Oh thank God." Eli grabbed him and rolled. "I'm dying over here."

"You want to fuck me?" Alanso squirmed on his belly. Though the pillow obscured half of his face, the other half darkened. With need, embarrassment, or both, Eli couldn't quite tell.

Never again would he leave someone he cared for to wonder about their standing in his life or his heart. "So damn bad. I love you. I want you in every sense of the phrase."

"I want to be yours," Alanso whispered. "*Te amo, querido.*"

And though Eli had worried about the softer side of their affections, it didn't weird him out at all to drop a light kiss on Alanso's cheek. Maybe he deserved to take this man after all. He promised both of them he'd always respect and honor this bond, whatever they called it.

Stretched out over Al, Eli reached for the lube in the nightstand. He sat on his heels, with his thighs bracketing Alanso's. From there he was able to insert his fingers beneath the waistband of the briefs that hugged his boyfriend's sculpted ass, framing it to even greater perfection.

Thinking of Alanso like that sent shivers racing up and down Eli's spine and pumped his cock even fuller than it'd already been.

"I think I can feel traces of my come on you from before. Good boy for not washing it off. You liked it when I staked my claim, didn't you?" Eli rubbed his knuckles over the small of Alanso's back. Slightly sticky, they both moaned at the memory of how close they'd come to living their dream.

"*Mierda, sí!* No more almosts, Cobra." Alanso turned steely. "This time for real. All the way."

"I'm glad you agree." He smacked the ass laid out before him, slightly paler than the rest of Alanso's tan skin. After another spank he kneaded the quivering muscles, separating the cheeks just a little. "Because no chance in hell am I stopping now."

He retrieved the lube from the sheets and snapped open the cap. In the brightening space he still had some trouble seeing the transparent liquid. Alanso's hiss let him know when the cool gel hit bull's eye.

"You'll appreciate that in a minute." Eli grunted. "Trust me, I can still feel how deep your cock was in me when I move. Thick fucker too."

Alanso stilled. "Did I hurt you?"

"Not in a bad way." Eli grinned. "Behave and I might even let you do it again soon."

"I'm about to come just thinking about it." A groan tore from his parted lips.

"Oh no." Eli slicked his fingers then his cock before tossing the lube onto the bed. "I

178

want you good and fired up when I slide my cock into that tight ass."

"Not a problem." Alanso wedged his hand beneath his body to cup his hard-on. Even if he couldn't jerk himself in that position, he could apply some pressure. Maybe to squeeze the base of his shaft and prevent himself from tipping over the edge far too soon.

The angle of his hips presented his ass even more fully to Eli's roving hand. Cobra tucked his finger between those rock-hard cheeks and followed the valley between them to Alanso's hole.

They both shouted something unintelligible at the initial contact.

Eli sank inside his best friend, rubbing in tiny circles as he penetrated the rings of muscle protecting his rear. "Don't worry, *amigo*. I've done this before with chicks. If they can take me, you can."

"Just wish you'd hurry. All talk and no action, *pendejo*." Alanso grunted when Eli pushed harder, spearing deeper on each pump of his hand. "I'm no girl. Don't treat me like one."

"I don't doubt you can handle anything I have to dish out." Eli withdrew to shuck his own briefs. He groaned at the weight of his erection flopping free and the room temperature air on his hand, which felt downright icy after Alanso's core. He planted his knees on either side of Alanso's once again and tipped forward, shoving his hands beneath the guy's shoulders, cupping them in his palms to anchor his head mechanic while he roughly aligned their bodies. "But this is more to me than sex. Understand that or I stop right now."

Alanso gasped when Eli nuzzled him. "Wouldn't let you fuck me if it wasn't."

"You gave those guys in the woods a chance to touch what's mine." Eli had never experienced the burn of jealousy before. Never wanted to again.

"Practicing for you." Alanso rocked his ass backward. When the tip of Eli's cock wedged in perfect position for penetration, they both cursed.

"Do it. Do me." Alanso practically begged.

Eli hugged him and said, "My pleasure."

He began to forge inside Alanso, using steady pressure on the opening to his body.

At first he met with so much resistance, he wasn't sure he'd ever make it through. When he whispered, "Let me in. Please," Alanso relented.

Eli breached him.

Alanso's eyes flew open in the new dawn.

A beam of sunlight streaked through the window, illuminating his chocolate eyes as they widened. Eli advanced, joining them more fully. As Alanso's ass hugged inch after inch of Cobra's cock, he blanketed his lover with his body, hoping Al realized that Eli intended to have his back for life.

That hadn't changed, at least.

When he'd buried a significant portion of his shaft, he paused.

"No." Alanso bucked beneath him. "You'll give me everything or nothing at all."

"Jesus. Crazy Cuban. I'm just giving you a chance to adjust." Eli gritted his teeth to keep from riding like he yearned to.

"Ever notice patience is not my strong suit?" Alanso shoved against the bed. He thrust himself up over Eli's cock until they met abdomen to ass. Not a single molecule of air separated them.

Eli prayed he wouldn't embarrass himself by shooting before he'd even begun to really fuck. He thought about the model number of the new spark plugs he had to order tomorrow, and tried to figure up the total cost to distract himself from the pulsing of Alanso's fist-tight flesh.

The tang of iron made him realize he'd bitten his tongue again too.

Under control, barely, he reprimanded Alanso for nearly stealing his thunder. "If you do that again, I'll make you wait a year before

I fuck you next. I'd like to give you a proper ride, if you don't mind. Don't fucking sabotage me."

"Fancy shit later." Alanso moaned when Eli withdrew then slammed deep.

"You're that close, are you?" Eli grinned when he recognized the burn of impending orgasm in his friend's tone, the set of his jaw and the dazed quality to his stare.

"*Estoy en el borde. Date prisa.*"

"No fucking idea what you're saying, but you sound sexy as hell." Eli dropped down to nip Alanso's lip.

Al turned his head and whimpered when Eli began to ply his mouth with tender kisses, even as his hips alternated liquid glides with pounding strokes. He tried to make it good, but primal instinct led him to mix a claim with his promises.

"I'm not coming without you, Alanso." Eli spoke low and firm. "We're in this together."

"Can't, Cobra." He pounded the mattress. "Hurts so good. Need more."

"I said let go." Eli refused to relent.

Alanso shivered beneath him now, in ecstasy and maybe some pain from the intensity of their sharing. Refusing to be denied, Eli rolled to his side. He tipped Alanso with him, still joined. His hand roamed down the solid slab of his friend's chest, pausing to tug on the piercings that decorated his nipples.

Alanso shouted Eli's name.

"What do you want, *amigo*?" He walked his hand lower, all the while still plowing into Alanso from behind. The flex of his abs began to burn at the awkward angle and he knew he couldn't keep it up forever. Luckily, neither of them would need very long. "This?"

His fingers closed around Alanso's cock. The moment they did, the smaller man howled. He fucked forward into Eli's fist. His ass grew tighter, practically strangling Eli's cock.

"Yes. Yes," Eli chanted. "Come for me. Let me watch you shoot while I'm fucking buried in you. Deep as I can get."

He aimed the head of Alanso's cock at the man's tattoo-covered chest. He wanted proof that his lover enjoyed their fucking as much, or more, than he did. And Al didn't disappoint.

Alanso roared Eli's name.

He stiffened in Cobra's arms until he might have shattered.

And then he did. His ass locked over Eli's erection and the first jet of come launched from his cock. Instead of the target Eli had intended—his pecs—he overshot the landing pad, spraying Eli on the chin and across his smile.

Alanso stared at him with wide eyes as he spasmed, adding to the mess on Eli's lips.

Making sure neither of them would ever forget this moment or how fully he pledged himself to the man coming apart in his arms, Eli opened his mouth. He swiped a droplet from the corner of his lips with his tongue and ingested the silky substance.

The taste of Alanso, and the utter devotion in the man's stare, combined to trigger his own orgasm. He crushed his mouth over Alanso's as best he could given the angle. Somehow they made it work. They were meant to fit together.

Their tongues parried as Eli filled Alanso's ass with gush after gush of come.

And still Alanso's cock jerked, as if the pleasure Eli pumped into him enhanced his lingering climax. He shook and cursed until fluid dribbled from his sated cock, as though it wished it had more to pump out.

Insatiable, Eli speared into the steaming, now sloppy paradise he claimed a few more times, until all of his strength leeched away along with doubt, fear and delays.

This is what he'd been made for.

"Cobra," Alanso whispered.

"Yeah?" He shivered when their positions and his softening cock meant he slipped free of Alanso's body sooner than he would have liked.

"That was...everything." His respiration remained uneven and labored.

"For me too." Eli traced the streaks of come on Alanso's ripped abdomen. He smeared them over the ridges and valleys of muscle there before lifting his fingers to his friend's lips. The smaller man didn't hesitate before taking them into his mouth and suckling them like a pacifier.

"This is the beginning, Alanso. Another start," Eli whispered against his lover's neck, just below the small spacer in his earlobe. "I promise you, no matter where the road leads from here, we'll drive it together. *I* will never leave you."

"Hot Rods for life." Alanso nodded and smiled, a little shy and a lot hopeful.

"Hell yeah," Eli agreed.

Just then Pitbull's "Secret Admirer" warred with AC/DC's "Dirty Deeds" as Cobra and Alanso got synchronized texts.

"Sally!" Alanso cried out. "Not bad news. Not now."

"No." Eli refused to believe that. Especially when he knew her so well. "She's really fucking early. She had to have set a speeding record in at least one of those states. Driving like a bat out of hell."

He reached across Alanso to retrieve his phone and punch in a response to Joe's note telling them to stand down and wait. The crew had Eli and Alanso's girl. It was going to be a long two weeks before they gave her back.

At least Cobra had Alanso to help him relax.

"Tell Joe to go ahead and spank her after all." Alanso's eyes drifted shut as relief mingled with exhaustion.

It'd been one hell of a day for them all.

As sunlight spilled into their nest, Eli smiled and burrowed close to his right-hand man. "I'll save that for us. All of us. *When* she comes home. We'll be ready and waiting."

"I do love you, *cabrón*." Alanso smirked without opening his eyes.

"Then shut up and let me sleep." Eli didn't have to wait more than ten seconds before light snores lulled him into dreamland. When Alanso snuffled and snugged closer, he knew the other man understood, if not heard, his drowsy whisper, "I love you too. I always have."

THE ADVENTURES DON'T END HERE! KEEP READING...

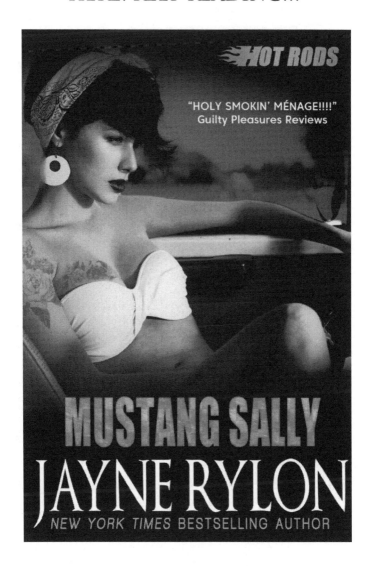

Salome "Sally" Rider is flooring the gas pedal of her pink '69 Mustang, desperate to outrun the memory of two of her fellow mechanics getting busy with some bar skank on the hood of a classic car. On her custom paint job.

For years her emotions have withered while her lost boys, her Hot Rods, have grown closer than brothers. Maybe some down time with the Powertools sexperts will help her figure out why Eli and Alanso went looking for some strange, when Sally was waiting right at the ends of their grease-smudged noses.

Sally is dead wrong about what she thought she saw, and Eli "King Cobra" London and the rest of the thoroughly rattled Hot Rods are determined prove it. They'll show her in the sexiest possible way that she's not merely an interchangeable part in their well-oiled machine.

Yet just as Eli gets up the nerve to make a very indecent proposal, a ghost rises from her painful past. Threatening to slam the brakes on their future before they can get it in gear.

EXCERPT FROM MUSTANG SALLY, HOT RODS BOOK 2

The stainless steel skeletal butterfly on her fob rattled against her car and house keys as she ascended the open-backed stairs at the rear of the industrial building. The two slivers of metal reminded her of all the stakes. Her home. Her car. Her Hot Rods, who'd given her the trinket, binding them together on the first Christmas she'd spent with them a decade ago.

The badass butterfly had been her signature logo ever since, painted on each piece she created. That included her own Mustang and every other vehicle the Hot Rods obsessed over. Why did they mean so much to her if she didn't matter a bit to them? Their sexy bodies and friendship had obviously warped her judgment.

When she went to fit her key in the lock, the door at the top of the stairs swung open. Had they forgotten to pull it closed? A bunch of them had grown up on the streets or in places a hell of a lot less protected. Security wasn't something they slacked off on despite the relative safety of Middletown.

"Um, hello?" A shiver ran down her spine. Something wasn't right. When a skitter of motion flickered through her unadjusted peripheral vision, she didn't hesitate.

Using the self-defense instruction Roman had often given her, she balled her fist and swung at the shadow rapidly encroaching on her. Her knuckles connected with flesh. Holy crap.

It hurt, but not enough to keep her from landing a second punch to someplace softer. Who the hell was in their house? In the dark? Had they hurt her Hot Rods?

She'd rip them apart with her bare hands if they had.

"Oompf." The grunt sounded somewhat familiar. But Sally wasn't sure the person she'd decked was Eli until he hollered, "Guys! Turn the lights on."

Brightness flashed into existence, blinding Sally.

"Welcome home!" a chorus of male voices shouted, mostly together.

She nearly toppled onto her ass when fight or flight instincts propelled her headlong into the bizarre scene in front of her. Eli bent in half, clutching his abdomen with one hand and his face with the other. Alanso stood slightly behind him, eyes wide and mouth hanging open.

After them, a mass of guys milled around with beers, ridiculous party hats, oversized balloons from the shop and an impressive assortment of snack cakes that looked like they might have come from the convenience section of the gas station.

"Uh-oh." She dropped her keys.

Holden cracked up first. He adored mischief. This one might go down in the history books as the most awkward greeting of all time. "Well, he had it coming."

"Somebody hand me some paper towels." Alanso rushed to Eli's side. A trickle of blood spattered onto the floor.

"I'm fine. It's fine." Eli tried to shake it off. He lifted his head and ignored any discomfort he might be in. Peeking at her from the slivers of his eyes not scrunched in pain, he said, "Hey, there."

"Oh my God." Sally's shoulders drooped. "I'm so sorry. I thought... It was dark. I didn't think you were home. The door was unlocked."

"And you still came inside. By yourself?" Roman practically growled at her.

"She can hold her own." Eli surprised her by taking her side. He pressed the napkin, which Carver had offered, to his face and tipped his head back as he pinched the bridge of his nose.

And just like that, Sally couldn't handle any more. She didn't give a damn if they thought less of her. She'd always made a point of showing no weakness around the gang of mechanics. Or at least she'd tried. But tonight there was no stopping the flood of tears that swept over her.

"Shh." Alanso was there in an instant. He smelled nice, like grease and the cinnamon gum he liked. Breathing deep, she didn't resist as he wrapped her in his stocky arms and fitted her to his chest. "It'll take a hell of a lot more than a bop on the nose to put King Cobra in his place. It's okay. We shouldn't have startled you like that. Hijo de puta, why do we keep screwing things up?"

"No, no." She squirmed in his hold, wanting to peek over his shoulder to verify she hadn't imagined the effort they'd gone to. They cared. They'd missed her. Maybe even a fraction as much as she'd pined for them. "It's perfect. Amazing. I ruined things. Again."

"I wouldn't say that, Sally." Kaige raised his beer in her direction. "I'm having a wicked good time. Nice hook, by the way."

A weak smile began to turn her frown upside down. Her eyes skipped over his bold tattoos and his golden dreads to the older man standing quietly at the rear of the gang.

King Cobra's dad, Tom, nodded in her direction, then held his hands up so that his curled fingers made the top of a heart and his thumbs pointed together, completing the shape. The gesture alone brought fresh tears to her eyes.

Damn, this wasn't going to be pretty.

She let go of Alanso just long enough to flash the sign in return.

Together she and the engine tuner faced Eli.

"It's stopping. All cool. No worries." He crumpled the paper towel and jammed it in the back pocket of his jeans. "I missed you, Sally."

"I missed you too." She held out her arms. Both Eli and Alanso stepped into them. She hugged each of them with one arm and they mimicked her until the triangle was complete.

With the three of them bonded in their own private assembly, Eli whispered into her ear, "We have a lot to talk about. After the party. You. Me. Alanso. Please let me explain?"

She froze. The plan had been to charge in and hit them with her demands, both barrels. Would she still have the nerve to be so bold after an hour or two of hanging out, pretending all was normal when everything inside her had disintegrated and rearranged? And what about her unfinished business? She wouldn't have time to dive into it before the three of them hashed things out. Crap!

Is this how Alanso had felt when he'd returned from the guys' visit to the crew after Dave's accident? If so, she had no clue how he'd held it all together so long. His strength awed her. Just like it had when he'd burst inside that night a few weeks ago and announced he wanted to experiment with guys. She had to take a page from his book and be brave enough to share her desires. Otherwise, there was no hope of getting what she needed.

Sally kissed the bald guy's cheek as she rubbed his head. He nearly purred when she found the spot he loved so much. Then she turned to Eli to bestow the same peace offering on him. Though she'd kissed his cheek a million times in their lives, this time was different.

At the last instant, he turned his head.

They met lips on lips for the first time.

Sally's heart sputtered in her chest like the engine on one of their fresh finds. To finally touch him, like this, with intent to do more—it amazed her. He was gentle, more than she would have expected. His thumbs brushed her cheeks as his fingers buried in the long strands of her hair.

When her knees turned to motor oil, Alanso held her up, tucked tight to his frame.

He lifted her toward his best friend, allowed the man to feast at her mouth.

Eli's tongue traced her smile. He nibbled on her bottom lip while she tried to shake herself from the stunned trance his touch induced. She purred, then kissed him back, clutching both him and Alanso as they made out in front of all the witnesses that mattered.

ABOUT THE AUTHOR

Jayne Rylon is a *New York Times* and *USA Today* bestselling author. She received the 2011 RomanticTimes Reviewers' Choice Award for Best Indie Erotic Romance.

Her stories used to begin as daydreams in seemingly endless business meetings, but now she is a full-time author, who employs the skills she learned from her straight-laced corporate existence in the business of writing. She lives in Ohio with two cats and her husband, the infamous Mr. Rylon.

When she can escape her purple office, Jayne loves to travel the world, SCUBA dive, take pictures, avoid speeding tickets in her beloved Sky and—of course—read.